1001

Arabian

Nights

The Complete Adventures Of Sindbad, Aladdin And Ali Baba

Special Edition

Edited by
Shawn Conners

1001 Arabian Nights – The Complete Adventures of Sindbad, Aladdin, and Ali Baba – Special Edition

By Anonymous
Translated by Dr. Jonathan Scott
Edited by Shawn Conners

First Edition - September 2009

Published by
EL Paso Norte Press
El Paso, Texas

ISBN 10 1-934255-20-3
ISBN 13 978-193425520-9

Printed in the United States of America

Preface

The "Arabian Nights" was introduced to Europe in a French translation by Antoine Galland in 1704, and rapidly attained a unique popularity. There are even accounts of the translator being roused from sleep by bands of young men under his windows in Paris, importuning him to tell them another story.

The learned world at first refused to believe that Galland had not invented the tales. But he had really discovered an Arabic manuscript from sixteenth-century Egypt, and had consulted Oriental story-tellers. In spite of inaccuracies and loss of color, his twelve volumes long remained classic in France, and formed the basis of our popular translations.

A more accurate version, corrected from the Arabic, with a style admirably direct, easy, and simple, was published by Dr. Jonathan Scott in 1811. This is the text of the present edition.

The Moslems delight in stories, but are generally ashamed to show a literary interest in fiction. Hence the world's most delightful story book has come to us with but scant indications of its origin. Critical scholarship, however, has been able to reach fairly definite conclusions.

The reader will be interested to trace out for himself the similarities in the adventures of the two Persian queens, Scheherazade, and Esther of Bible story, which M. de Goeje has pointed out as indicating their original identity. There are two or three references in tenth-century Arabic literature to a Persian collection of tales, called The Thousand Nights, by the fascination of which the lady Scheherazade kept winning one more day's lease of life. A good many of the tales as we have them contain elements clearly indicating Persian or Hindu origin. But most of the stories, even those with scenes laid in

Persia or India, are thoroughly Mohammedan in thought, feeling, situation, and action.

The favorite scene is "the glorious city," ninth-century Bagdad, whose caliph, Haroun al Raschid, though a great king, and heir of still mightier men, is known to fame chiefly by the favor of these tales. But the contents (with due regard to the possibility of later insertions), references in other writings, and the dialect show that our Arabian Nights took form in Egypt very soon after the year 1450. The author, doubtless a professional teller of stories, was, like his Scheherazade, a person of extensive reading and faultless memory, fluent of speech, and ready on occasion to drop into poetry. The coarseness of the Arabic narrative, which does not appear in our translation, is characteristic of Egyptian society under the Mameluke sultans. It would have been tolerated by the subjects of the caliph in old Bagdad no more than by modern Christians.

More fascinating stories were never told. Though the oath of an Oriental was of all things the most sacred, and though Schah-riar had "bound himself by a solemn vow to marry a new wife every night, and command her to be strangled in the morning," we well believe that he forswore himself, and granted his bride a stay of execution until he could find out why the ten polite young gentlemen, all blind of the right eye, "having blackened themselves, wept and lamented, beating their heads and breasts, and crying continually, 'This is the fruit of our idleness and curiosity.'" To be sure, when the golden door has been opened, and the black horse has vanished with that vicious switch of his tail, we have a little feeling of having been "sold,"--a feeling which great art never gives. But we are in the best of humor; for were we not warned all along against just this foible of curiosity, and is not the story-teller smiling inscrutably and advising us to be thankful that we at least still have our two good eyes?

Beside the story interest, the life and movement of the tales, the spirits that enter and set their own precedents, there is for us the charm of mingling with men so different from ourselves: men adventurous but never strenuous, men of many tribulations but no perplexities. Fantastic, magnificent, extravagant, beautiful, gloriously colored, humorous--was ever book of such infinite contrasts?

Table
Of
Contents

The Story of Aladdin And His Wonderful Lamp

In one of the large and rich cities of China there once lived a tailor named Mustapha. He was very poor. He could hardly, by his daily labor, maintain himself and his family, which consisted only of his wife and a son.

His son, who was called Aladdin, was a very careless and idle fellow. He was disobedient to his father and mother, and would go out early in the morning and stay out all day, playing in the streets and public places with idle children of his own age.

When he was old enough to learn a trade his father took him into his own shop, and taught him how to use his needle; but all his father's endeavors to keep him to his work were vain, for no sooner was his back turned than the boy was gone for that day. Mustapha chastised him, but Aladdin was incorrigible, and his father, to his great grief, was forced to abandon him to his idleness. He was so much troubled about him, that he fell sick and died in a few months.

Aladdin, who was now no longer restrained by the fear of a father, gave himself over entirely to his idle habits, and was never out of the streets from his companions. This course he followed till he was fifteen years old, without giving his mind to any useful pursuit, or the least reflection on what would become of him. As he was one day playing in the street with his evil associates, according to custom, a stranger passing by stood to observe him.

1

This stranger was a sorcerer, known as the African magician, as he had been but two days arrived from Africa, his native country.

The African magician, observing in Aladdin's countenance something which assured him that he was a fit boy for his purpose, inquired his name and history of his companions. When he had learned all he desired to know, he went up to him, and taking him aside from his comrades, said, "Child, was not your father called Mustapha the tailor?"

"Yes, sir," answered the boy, "but he has been dead a long time."

At these words the African magician threw his arms about Aladdin's neck, and kissed him several times, with tears in his eyes, saying, "I am your uncle. Your worthy father was my own brother. I knew you at first sight, you are so like him."

Then he gave Aladdin a handful of small money, saying, "Go, my son, to your mother. Give my love to her, and tell her that I will visit her to-morrow, that I may see where my good brother lived so long, and ended his days."

Aladdin ran to his mother, overjoyed at the money his uncle had given him.

"Mother," said he, "have I an uncle?"

"No, child," replied his mother, "you have no uncle by your father's side or mine."

"I am just now come," said Aladdin, "from a man who says he is my uncle, and my father's brother. He cried, and kissed me, when I told him my father was dead, and gave me money, sending his love to you, and promising to come and pay you a visit, that he may see the house my father lived and died in."

"Indeed, child," replied the mother, "your father had no brother, nor have you an uncle."

The next day the magician found Aladdin playing in another part of the town, and embracing him as before, put two pieces of gold into his hand, and said to him, "Carry this, child, to your mother. Tell her that I will come and see her to-night, and bid her get us something for supper. But first show me the house where you live."

Aladdin showed the African magician the house, and carried the two pieces of gold to his mother, who went out and bought provisions; and considering she wanted various utensils, borrowed them of her neighbors. She spent the whole day in preparing the supper; and at night, when it was ready, said to her son, "Perhaps the stranger knows not how to find our house; go and bring him, if you meet with him."

Aladdin was just ready to go, when the magician knocked at the door, and came in loaded with wine and all sorts of fruits, which he brought for a dessert. After he had given what he brought into Aladdin's hands, he saluted his mother, and desired her to show him the place where his brother Mustapha used to sit on the sofa; and when she had so done, he fell down, and kissed it several times, crying out, with tears in his eyes, "My poor brother! how unhappy am I, not to have come soon enough to give you one last embrace!"

Aladdin's mother desired him to sit down in the same place, but he declined.

"No," said he, "I shall not do that; but give me leave to sit opposite to it, that although I see not the master of a family so dear to me, I may at least behold the place where he used to sit."

When the magician had made choice of a place, and sat down, he began to enter into discourse with Aladdin's mother.

"My good sister," said he, "do not be surprised at your never having seen me all the time you have been married to my brother Mustapha of happy memory. I have been forty years absent from this country, which is my native place as well as my late brother's. During that time I have traveled into the Indies, Persia, Arabia, and Syria, and afterward crossed over into Africa, where I took up my abode in Egypt. At last, as it is natural for a man, I was desirous to see my native country again, and to embrace my dear brother; and finding I had strength enough to undertake so long a journey, I made the necessary preparations, and set out. Nothing ever afflicted me so much as hearing of my brother's death. But God be praised for all things! It is a comfort for me to find, as it were, my brother in a son, who has his most remarkable features."

The African magician, perceiving that the widow wept at the remembrance of her husband, changed the conversation, and turning toward her son, asked him, "What business do you follow? Are you of any trade?"

At this question the youth hung down his head, and was not a little abashed when his mother answered, "Aladdin is an idle fellow. His father, when alive, strove all he could to teach him his trade, but could not succeed; and since his death, notwithstanding all I can say to him, he does nothing but idle away his time in the streets, as you saw him, without considering he is no longer a child; and if you do not make him ashamed of it, I despair of his ever coming to any good. For my part, I am resolved, one of these days, to turn him out of doors, and let him provide for himself."

After these words, Aladdin's mother burst into tears; and the magician said, "This is not well, nephew; you must think of helping yourself, and getting your livelihood. There are many sorts of trades; perhaps you do not like your father's, and would prefer another; I will endeavor to help you. If you have no mind to learn any handicraft, I will take a shop for you, furnish it with all sorts of fine stuffs and linens; and then with the money you make of them you can lay in fresh goods, and live in an honorable way. Tell me freely what you think of my proposal; you shall always find me ready to keep my word."

This plan just suited Aladdin, who hated work. He told the magician he had a greater inclination to that business than to any other, and that he should be much obliged to him for his kindness. "Well, then," said the African magician, "I will carry you with me to-morrow, clothe you as handsomely as the best merchants in the city, and afterward we will open a shop as I mentioned."

The widow, after his promise of kindness to her son, no longer doubted that the magician was her husband's brother. She thanked him for his good intentions; and after having exhorted Aladdin to render himself worthy of his uncle's favor, she served up supper, at which they talked of several indifferent matters; and then the magician took his leave and retired.

He came again the next day, as he had promised, and took Aladdin with him to a merchant, who sold all sorts of clothes for different ages and ranks, ready-made, and a variety of fine stuffs, and bade Aladdin choose those he preferred, which he paid for.

When Aladdin found himself so handsomely equipped, he returned his uncle thanks, who thus addressed him: "As you are soon to be a merchant, it is proper you should frequent these shops, and become acquainted with them."

He then showed him the largest and finest mosques, carried him to the khans or inns where the merchants and travelers lodged, and afterward to the sultan's palace, where he had free access; and at last brought him to his own khan, where, meeting with some merchants he had become acquainted with since his arrival, he gave them a treat, to bring them and his pretended nephew acquainted.

This entertainment lasted till night, when Aladdin would have taken leave of his uncle to go home. The magician would not let him go by himself, but conducted him to his mother, who, as soon as she saw him so well dressed, was transported with joy, and bestowed a thousand blessings upon the magician.

Early the next morning the magician called again for Aladdin, and said he would take him to spend that day in the country, and on the next he would purchase the shop. He then led him out at one of the gates of the city, to some magnificent palaces, to each of which belonged beautiful gardens, into which anybody might enter. At every building he came to he asked Aladdin if he did not think it fine; and the youth was ready to answer, when any one presented itself, crying out, "Here is a finer house, uncle, than any we have yet seen."

By this artifice the cunning magician led Aladdin some way into the country; and as he meant to carry him farther, to execute his design, pretending to be tired, he took an opportunity to sit down in one of the gardens, on the brink of a fountain of clear water which discharged itself by a lion's mouth of bronze into a basin.

"Come, nephew," said he, "you must be weary as well as I. Let us rest ourselves, and we shall be better able to pursue our walk."

The magician next pulled from his girdle a handkerchief with cakes and fruit, and during this short repast he exhorted his nephew to leave off bad company, and to seek that of wise and prudent men, to improve by their conversation. "For," said he, "you will soon be at man's estate, and you cannot too early begin to imitate their example."

When they had eaten as much as they liked, they got up, and pursued their walk through gardens separated from one another only by small ditches, which marked out the limits without interrupting the communication; so great was the confidence the inhabitants reposed in each other.

By this means the African magician drew Aladdin insensibly beyond the gardens, and crossed the country, till they nearly reached the mountains.

At last they arrived between two mountains of moderate height and equal size, divided by a narrow valley, where the magician intended to execute the design that had brought him from Africa to China.

"We will go no farther now," said he to Aladdin. "I will show you here some extraordinary things, which, when you have seen, you will thank me for; but while I strike a light, gather up all the loose dry sticks you can see, to kindle a fire with."

Aladdin found so many dried sticks that he soon collected a great heap. The magician presently set them on fire; and when they were in a blaze he threw in some incense, pronouncing several magical words, which Aladdin did not understand.

He had scarcely done so when the earth opened just before the magician, and disclosed a stone with a brass ring fixed in it. Aladdin was so frightened that he would have run away, but the magician caught hold of him, and gave him such a box on the ear that he knocked him down. Aladdin got up trembling, and, with tears in his eyes, said to the magician, "What have I done, uncle, to be treated in this severe manner?"

"I am your uncle," answered the magician; "I supply the place of your father, and you ought to make no reply. But, child," added he, softening, "do not be afraid; for I shall not ask anything of you, but that, if you obey me punctually, you will reap the advantages which I intend you. Know, then, that under this stone there is hidden a treasure, destined to be yours, and which will make you richer than the greatest monarch in the world. No person but yourself is permitted to lift this stone, or enter the cave; so you must punctually execute what I may command, for it is a matter of great consequence both to you and to me."

Aladdin, amazed at all he saw and heard, forgot what was past, and rising said, "Well, uncle, what is to be done? Command me. I am ready to obey."

"I am overjoyed, child," said the African magician, embracing him. "Take hold of the ring, and lift up that stone."

"Indeed, uncle," replied Aladdin, "I am not strong enough; you must help me."

"You have no occasion for my assistance," answered the magician; "if I help you, we shall be able to do nothing. Take hold of the ring, and lift it up; you will find it will come easily." Aladdin did as the magician bade him, raised the stone with ease, and laid it on one side.

When the stone was pulled up there appeared a staircase about three or four feet deep, leading to a door.

"Descend those steps, my son," said the African magician, "and open that door. It will lead you into a palace, divided into three great halls. In each of these you will see four large brass cisterns placed on each side, full of gold and silver; but take care you do not meddle with them. Before you enter the first hall, be sure to tuck up your robe, wrap it about you, and then pass through the second into the third without stopping. Above all things, have a care that you do not touch the walls so much as with your clothes; for if you do, you will die instantly. At the end of the third hall you will find a door which opens into a garden planted with fine trees loaded with fruit. Walk directly across the garden to a terrace, where you will see a niche before you, and in that niche a lighted lamp. Take the lamp down and put it out. When you have thrown away the wick and poured out the liquor, put it in your waistband and bring it to me. Do not be afraid that the liquor will spoil your clothes, for it is not oil, and the lamp will be dry as soon as it is thrown out."

After these words the magician drew a ring off his finger, and put it on one of Aladdin's, saying, "It is a talisman against all evil, so long as you obey me. Go, therefore, boldly, and we shall both be rich all our lives."

Aladdin descended the steps, and, opening the door, found the three halls just as the African magician had described. He went through them with all the precaution the fear of death could inspire, crossed the garden without stopping, took down the lamp from the niche, threw out the wick and the liquor, and, as the magician had desired, put it in his waistband. But as he came down from the terrace, seeing it was perfectly dry, he stopped in the garden to observe the trees, which were loaded with extraordinary fruit of different colors on each tree. Some bore fruit entirely white, and some clear and transparent as crystal; some pale red, and others deeper; some green, blue, and purple, and others yellow; in short, there was fruit of all colors. The white were pearls; the clear and transparent, diamonds; the deep red, rubies; the paler, ballas rubies; the green, emeralds; the blue, turquoises; the purple, amethysts; and the yellow, sapphires. Aladdin, ignorant of their value, would have preferred figs, or grapes, or pomegranates; but as he had his uncle's permission, he resolved to gather some of every sort. Having filled the two new purses his uncle had bought for him with his clothes, he wrapped some up in the skirts of his vest, and crammed his bosom as full as it could hold.

Aladdin, having thus loaded himself with riches of which he knew not the value, returned through the three halls with the utmost precaution, and soon arrived at the mouth of the cave, where the African magician awaited him with the utmost impatience.

As soon as Aladdin saw him, he cried out, "Pray, uncle, lend me your hand, to help me out."

"Give me the lamp first," replied the magician; "it will be troublesome to you."

"Indeed, uncle," answered Aladdin, "I cannot now; but I will as soon as I am up."

The African magician was determined that he would have the lamp before he would help him up; and Aladdin, who had encumbered himself so much with his fruit that he could not well get at it, refused to give it to him till he was out of the cave. The African magician, provoked at this obstinate refusal, flew into a passion, threw a little of his incense into the fire, and pronounced two magical words, when the stone which had closed the mouth of the staircase moved into its place, with the earth over it in the same manner as it lay at the arrival of the magician and Aladdin.

This action of the magician plainly revealed to Aladdin that he was no uncle of his, but one who designed him evil. The truth was that he had learned from his magic books the secret and the value of this wonderful lamp, the owner of which would be made richer than any earthly ruler, and hence his journey to China. His art had also told him that he was not permitted to take it himself, but must receive it as a voluntary gift from the hands of another person. Hence he employed young Aladdin, and hoped by a mixture of kindness and authority to make him obedient to his word and will. When he found that his attempt had failed, he set out to return to Africa, but avoided the town, lest any person who had seen him leave in company with Aladdin should make inquiries after the youth.

Aladdin, being suddenly enveloped in darkness, cried, and called out to his uncle to tell him he was ready to give him the lamp. But in vain, since his cries could not be heard.

He descended to the bottom of the steps, with a design to get into the palace, but the door, which was opened before by enchantment, was now shut by the same means. He then redoubled his cries and tears, sat down on the steps without any hopes of ever seeing light again, and in an expectation of passing from the present darkness to a speedy death.

In this great emergency he said, "There is no strength or power but in the great and high God"; and in joining his hands to pray he rubbed the ring which the magician had put on his finger. Immediately a genie of frightful aspect appeared, and said, "What wouldst thou have? I am ready to obey thee. I serve him who possesses the ring on thy finger; I, and the other slaves of that ring."

At another time Aladdin would have been frightened at the sight of so extraordinary a figure, but the danger he was in made him answer without hesitation, "Whoever thou art, deliver me from this place." He had no sooner spoken these words than he found himself on the very spot where the magician had last left him, and no sign of cave or opening, nor disturbance of the earth. Returning thanks to God for being once more in the world, he made the best of his way home. When he got within his mother's door, joy at seeing her and weakness for want of sustenance made him so faint that he remained for a long time as dead. As soon as he recovered, he related to his mother all that had happened to him, and they were both very vehement in their complaints of the cruel magician.

Aladdin slept very soundly till late the next morning, when the first thing he said to his mother was, that he wanted something to eat, and wished she would give him his breakfast.

"Alas! child," said she, "I have not a bit of bread to give you; you ate up all the provisions I had in the house yesterday; but I have a little cotton which I have spun; I will go and sell it, and buy bread and something for our dinner."

"Mother," replied Aladdin, "keep your cotton for another time, and give me the lamp I brought home with me yesterday. I will go and sell it, and the money I shall get for it will serve both for breakfast and dinner, and perhaps supper too."

Aladdin's mother took the lamp and said to her son, "Here it is, but it is very dirty. If it were a little cleaner I believe it would bring something more."

She took some fine sand and water to clean it. But she had no sooner begun to rub it, than in an instant a hideous genie of gigantic size appeared before her, and said to her in a voice of thunder, "What wouldst thou have? I am ready to obey thee as thy slave, and the slave of all those who have that lamp in their hands; I, and the other slaves of the lamp."

Aladdin's mother, terrified at the sight of the genie, fainted; when Aladdin, who had seen such a phantom in the cavern, snatched the lamp out of his mother's hand, and said to the genie boldly, "I am hungry. Bring me something to eat."

The genie disappeared immediately, and in an instant returned with a large silver tray, holding twelve covered dishes of the same metal, which contained the most delicious viands; six large white bread cakes on two plates, two flagons of wine, and two silver cups. All these he placed upon a carpet and disappeared; this was done before Aladdin's mother recovered from her swoon.

Aladdin had fetched some water, and sprinkled it in her face to recover her. Whether that or the smell of the meat effected her cure, it was not long before she came to herself.

"Mother," said Aladdin, "be not afraid. Get up and eat. Here is what will put you in heart, and at the same time satisfy my extreme hunger."

His mother was much surprised to see the great tray, twelve dishes, six loaves, the two flagons and cups, and to smell the savory odor which exhaled from the dishes.

"Child," said she, "to whom are we obliged for this great plenty and liberality? Has the sultan been made acquainted with our poverty, and had compassion on us?"

"It is no matter, mother," said Aladdin. "Let us sit down and eat; for you have almost as much need of a good breakfast as I myself. When we have done, I will tell you."

Accordingly, both mother and son sat down and ate with the better relish as the table was so well furnished. But all the time

The Story of Aladdin

Aladdin's mother could not forbear looking at and admiring the tray and dishes, though she could not judge whether they were silver or any other metal, and the novelty more than the value attracted her attention.

The mother and son sat at breakfast till it was dinner time, and then they thought it would be best to put the two meals together. Yet, after this they found they should have enough left for supper, and two meals for the next day.

When Aladdin's mother had taken away and set by what was left, she went and sat down by her son on the sofa, saying, "I expect now that you will satisfy my impatience, and tell me exactly what passed between the genie and you while I was in a swoon."

He readily complied with her request.

She was in as great amazement at what her son told her as at the appearance of the genie, and said to him, "But, son, what have we to do with genies? I never heard that any of my acquaintance had ever seen one. How came that vile genie to address himself to me, and not to you, to whom he had appeared before in the cave?"

"Mother," answered Aladdin, "the genie you saw is not the one who appeared to me. If you remember, he that I first saw called himself the slave of the ring on my finger; and this you saw, called himself the slave of the lamp you had in your hand; but I believe you did not hear him, for I think you fainted as soon as he began to speak."

15

"What!" cried the mother, "was your lamp then the occasion of that cursed genie's addressing himself to me rather than to you? Ah! my son, take it out of my sight, and put it where you please. I had rather you would sell it than run the hazard of being frightened to death again by touching it; and if you would take my advice, you would part also with the ring, and not have anything to do with genies, who, as our prophet has told us, are only devils."

"With your leave, mother," replied Aladdin, "I shall now take care how I sell a lamp which may be so serviceable both to you and me. That false and wicked magician would not have undertaken so long a journey to secure this wonderful lamp if he had not known its value to exceed that of gold and silver. And since we have honestly come by it, let us make a profitable use of it, without making any great show and exciting the envy and jealousy of our neighbors. However, since the genies frighten you so much, I will take it out of your sight, and put it where I may find it when I want it. The ring I cannot resolve to part with; for without that you had never seen me again; and though I am alive now, perhaps, if it were gone, I might not be so some moments hence. Therefore I hope you will give me leave to keep it, and to wear it always on my finger."

Aladdin's mother replied that he might do what he pleased; for her part, she would have nothing to do with genies, and never say anything more about them.

By the next night they had eaten all the provisions the genie had brought; and the next day Aladdin, who could not bear the thought of hunger, putting one of the silver dishes under his vest, went out early to sell it. Addressing himself to a Jew whom he met in the streets, he took him aside, and pulling out the plate, asked him if he would buy it.

The cunning Jew took the dish, examined it, and as soon as he found that it was good silver, asked Aladdin at how much he valued it.

Aladdin, who had never been used to such traffic, told him he would trust to his judgment and honor. The Jew was somewhat confounded at this plain dealing; and doubting whether Aladdin understood the material or the full value of what he offered to sell, took a piece of gold out of his purse and gave it him, though it was but the sixtieth part of the worth of the plate. Aladdin, taking the money very eagerly, retired with so much haste that the Jew, not content with the exorbitancy of his profit, was vexed he had not penetrated into his ignorance, and was going to run after him, to endeavor to get some change out of the piece of gold. But the boy ran so fast, and had got so far, that it would have been impossible to overtake him.

Before Aladdin went home he called at a baker's, bought some cakes of bread, changed his money, and on his return gave the rest to his mother, who went and purchased provisions enough to last them some time. After this manner they lived, until Aladdin had sold the twelve dishes singly, as necessity pressed, to the Jew, for the same money; who, after the first time, durst not offer him less, for fear of losing so good a bargain. When he had sold the last dish, he had recourse to the tray, which weighed ten times as much as the dishes, and would have carried it to his old purchaser, but that it was too large and cumbersome; therefore he was obliged to bring him home with him to his mother's, where, after the Jew had examined the weight of the tray, he laid down ten pieces of gold, with which Aladdin was very well satisfied.

When all the money was spent, Aladdin had recourse again to the lamp. He took it in his hands, looked for the part where his mother had rubbed it with the sand, and rubbed it also. The genie immediately appeared, and said, "What wouldst thou have? I am ready to obey thee as thy slave, and the slave of all those who have that lamp in their hands; I, and the other slaves of the lamp."

"I am hungry," said Aladdin. "Bring me something to eat."

The genie disappeared, and presently returned with a tray holding the same number of covered dishes as before, set it down, and vanished.

As soon as Aladdin found that their provisions were again expended, he took one of the dishes, and went to look for his Jew chapman. But as he was passing by a goldsmith's shop, the goldsmith perceiving him, called to him, and said, "My lad, I imagine that you have something to sell to the Jew, whom I often see you visit. Perhaps you do not know that he is the greatest rogue even among the Jews. I will give you the full worth of what you have to sell, or I will direct you to other merchants who will not cheat you."

This offer induced Aladdin to pull his plate from under his vest and show it to the goldsmith. At first sight he perceived that it was made of the finest silver, and asked if he had sold such as that to the Jew. When Aladdin told him he had sold him twelve such, for a piece of gold each, "What a villain!" cried the goldsmith. "But," added he, "my son, what is past cannot be recalled. By showing you the value of this plate, which is of the finest silver we use in our shops, I will let you see how much the Jew has cheated you."

The goldsmith took a pair of scales, weighed the dish, and assured him that his plate would fetch by weight sixty pieces of gold, which he offered to pay down immediately.

Aladdin thanked him for his fair dealing, and never after went to any other person.

Though Aladdin and his mother had an inexhaustible treasure in their lamp, and might have had whatever they wished for, yet they lived with the same frugality as before, and it may easily be supposed that the money for which Aladdin had sold the dishes and tray was sufficient to maintain them some time.

During this interval, Aladdin frequented the shops of the principal merchants, where they sold cloth of gold and silver, linens, silk stuffs, and jewelry, and, oftentimes joining in their conversation, acquired a knowledge of the world, and a desire to improve himself. By his acquaintance among the jewelers, he came to know that the fruits which he had gathered when he took the lamp were, instead of colored glass, stones of inestimable value; but he had the prudence not to mention this to any one, not even to his mother.

One day as Aladdin was walking about the town he heard an order proclaimed, commanding the people to shut up their shops and houses, and keep within doors while the Princess Buddir al Buddoor, the sultan's daughter, went to the bath and returned.

This proclamation inspired Aladdin with eager desire to see the princess's face, which he determined to gratify by placing himself behind the door of the bath, so that he could not fail to see her face.

Aladdin had not long concealed himself before the princess came. She was attended by a great crowd of ladies, slaves, and mutes, who walked on each side and behind her. When she came within three or four paces of the door of the bath, she took off her veil, and gave Aladdin an opportunity of a full view of her face.

The princess was a noted beauty; her eyes were large, lively, and sparkling; her smile bewitching; her nose faultless; her mouth small; her lips vermilion. It is not therefore surprising that Aladdin, who had never before seen such a blaze of charms, was dazzled and enchanted.

After the princess had passed by, and entered the bath, Aladdin quitted his hiding place, and went home. His mother perceived him to be more thoughtful and melancholy than usual, and asked what had happened to make him so, or if he were ill. He then told his mother all his adventure, and concluded by declaring, "I love the princess more than I can express, and am resolved that I will ask her in marriage of the sultan."

Aladdin's mother listened with surprise to what her son told her. When he talked of asking the princess in marriage, she laughed aloud.

"Alas! child," said she, "what are you thinking of? You must be mad to talk thus."

"I assure you, mother," replied Aladdin, "that I am not mad, but in my right senses. I foresaw that you would reproach me with folly and extravagance; but I must tell you once more that I am resolved to demand the princess of the sultan in marriage; nor do I despair of success. I have the slaves of the lamp and of the ring to help me, and you know how powerful their aid is. And I have another secret to tell you; those pieces of glass, which I got from the trees in the garden of the subterranean palace, are jewels of inestimable value, and fit for the greatest monarchs. All the precious stones the jewelers have in Bagdad are not to be compared to mine for size or beauty; and I am sure that the offer of them will secure the favor of the sultan. You have a large porcelain dish fit to hold them; fetch it, and let us see how they will look, when we have arranged them according to their different colors."

Aladdin's mother brought the china dish. Then he took the jewels out of the two purses in which he had kept them, and placed them in order, according to his fancy. But the brightness and luster they emitted in the daytime, and the variety of the colors, so dazzled the eyes both of mother and son that they were astonished beyond measure. Aladdin's mother, emboldened by the sight of these rich jewels, and fearful lest her son should be guilty of greater extravagance, complied with his request, and promised to go early the next morning to the palace of the sultan. Aladdin rose before daybreak, awakened his mother, pressing her to go to the sultan's palace and to get admittance, if possible, before the grand minister, the other ministers, and the great officers of state went in to take their seats in the divan, where the sultan always attended in person.

Aladdin's mother took the china dish, in which they had put the jewels the day before, wrapped it in two fine napkins, and set forward for the sultan's palace. When she came to the gates the grand minister, the other ministers, and most distinguished lords of the court were just gone in; but notwithstanding the crowd of people was great, she got into the divan, a spacious hall, the entrance into which was very magnificent. She placed herself just before the sultan, and the grand minister and the great lords, who sat in council on his right and left hand. Several causes were called, according to their order, pleaded and adjudged, until the time the divan generally broke up, when the sultan, rising, returned to his apartment, attended by the grand minister; the other ministers and ministers of state then retired, as also did all those whose business had called them thither.

Aladdin's mother, seeing the sultan retire, and all the people depart, judged rightly that he would not sit again that day, and resolved to go home. On her arrival she said, with much simplicity, "Son, I have seen the sultan, and am very well persuaded he has seen me, too, for I placed myself just before him; but he was so much taken up with those who attended on all sides of him that I pitied him, and wondered at his patience. At last I believe he was heartily tired, for he rose up suddenly, and would not hear a great many who were ready prepared to speak to him, but went away, at which I was well pleased, for indeed I began to lose all patience, and was extremely fatigued with staying so long. But there is no harm done; I will go again to-morrow. Perhaps the sultan may not be so busy."

The next morning she repaired to the sultan's palace with the present as early as the day before; but when she came there, she found the gates of the divan shut. She went six times afterward on the days appointed, placed herself always directly before the sultan, but with as little success as the first morning.

On the sixth day, however, after the divan was broken up, when the sultan returned to his own apartment he said to his grand minister: "I have for some time observed a certain woman, who attends constantly every day that I give audience, with something wrapped up in a napkin; she always stands up from the beginning to the breaking up of the audience, and effects to place herself just before me. If this woman comes to our next audience, do not fail to call her, that I may hear what she has to say."

The grand minister made answer by lowering his hand, and then lifting it up above his head, signifying his willingness to lose it if he failed.

On the next audience day, when Aladdin's mother went to the divan, and placed herself in front of the sultan as usual, the grand minister immediately called the chief of the mace-bearers, and pointing to her bade him bring her before the sultan. The old woman at once followed the mace-bearer, and when she reached the sultan, bowed her head down to the carpet which covered the platform of the throne, and remained in that posture until he bade her rise.

She had no sooner done so, than he said to her, "Good woman, I have observed you to stand many days from the beginning to the rising of the divan. What business brings you here?"

At these words, Aladdin's mother prostrated herself a second time, and when she arose, said, "Monarch of monarchs, I beg of you to pardon the boldness of my petition, and to assure me of your pardon and forgiveness."

"Well," replied the sultan, "I will forgive you, be it what it may, and no hurt shall come to you. Speak boldly."

When Aladdin's mother had taken all these precautions, for fear of the sultan's anger, she told him faithfully the errand on which her son had sent her, and the event which led to his making so bold a request in spite of all her remonstrances.

The sultan hearkened to this discourse without showing the least anger. But before he gave her any answer, he asked her what she had brought tied up in the napkin. She took the china dish which she had set down at the foot of the throne, untied it, and presented it to the sultan.

The sultan's amazement and surprise were inexpressible, when he saw so many large, beautiful, and valuable jewels collected in the dish. He remained for some time lost in admiration. At last, when he had recovered himself, he received the present from Aladdin's mother's hand, saying, "How rich, how beautiful!"

After he had admired and handled all the jewels one after another, he turned to his grand minister, and showing him the dish, said, "Behold, admire, wonder! And confess that your eyes never beheld jewels so rich and beautiful before."

The minister was charmed.

"Well," continued the sultan, "what sayest thou to such a present? Is it not worthy of the princess my daughter? And ought I not to bestow her on one who values her at so great a price?"

"I cannot but own," replied the grand minister, "that the present is worthy of the princess; but I beg of your majesty to grant me three months before you come to a final resolution. I hope, before that time, my son, whom you have regarded with your favor, will be able to make a nobler present than this Aladdin, who is an entire stranger to your majesty."

The sultan granted his request, and he said to the old woman, "Good woman, go home, and tell your son that I agree to the proposal you have made me; but I cannot marry the princess my daughter for three months. At the expiration of that time, come again."

Aladdin's mother returned home much more gratified than she had expected, and told her son with much joy the condescending answer she had received from the sultan's own mouth; and that she was to come to the divan again that day three months.

At hearing this news, Aladdin thought himself the most happy of all men, and thanked his mother for the pains she had taken in the affair, the good success of which was of so great importance to his peace that he counted every day, week, and even hour as it passed. When two of the three months were passed, his mother one evening, having no oil in the house, went out to buy some, and found a general rejoicing--the houses dressed with foliage, silks, and carpeting, and every one striving to show his joy according to his ability. The streets were crowded with officers in habits of ceremony, mounted on horses richly caparisoned, each attended by a great many footmen. Aladdin's mother asked the oil merchant what was the meaning of all this preparation of public festivity.

"Whence came you, good woman," said he, "that you don't know that the grand minister's son is to marry the Princess Buddir al Buddoor, the sultan's daughter, to-night? She will presently return from the bath; and these officers whom you see are to assist at the cavalcade to the palace, where the ceremony is to be solemnized."

Aladdin's mother, on hearing this news, ran home very quickly.

"Child," cried she, "you are undone! The sultan's fine promises will come to naught. This night the grand minister's son is to marry the Princess Buddir al Buddoor."

At this account Aladdin was thunderstruck. He bethought himself of the lamp, and of the genie who had promised to obey him; and without indulging in idle words against the sultan, the minister, or his son, he determined, if possible, to prevent the marriage.

When Aladdin had got into his chamber he took the lamp, and rubbing it in the same place as before, immediately the genie appeared, and said to him, "What wouldst thou have? I am ready to obey thee as thy slave; I, and the other slaves of the lamp."

"Hear me," said Aladdin. "Thou hast hitherto obeyed me, but now I am about to impose on thee a harder task. The sultan's daughter, who was promised me as my bride, is this night married to the son of the grand minister. Bring them both hither to me immediately they retire to their bedchamber."

"Master," replied the genie, "I obey you."

Aladdin supped with his mother as was their wont, and then went to his own apartment, and sat up to await the return of the genie, according to his commands.

In the meantime the festivities in honor of the princess's marriage were conducted in the sultan's palace with great magnificence. The ceremonies were at last brought to a conclusion, and the princess and the son of the minister retired to the bedchamber prepared for them. No sooner had they entered it, and dismissed their attendants, than the genie, the faithful slave of the lamp, to the great amazement and alarm of the bride and bridegroom took up the bed, and by an agency invisible to them, transported it in an instant into Aladdin's chamber, where he set it down.

"Remove the bridegroom," said Aladdin to the genie, "and keep him a prisoner till to-morrow dawn, and then return with him here." On Aladdin being left alone with the princess, he endeavored to assuage her fears, and explained to her the treachery practiced upon him by the sultan her father. He then laid himself down beside her, putting a drawn scimitar between them, to show that he was determined to secure her safety, and to treat her with the utmost possible respect. At break of day, the genie appeared at the appointed hour, bringing back the bridegroom, whom by breathing upon he had left motionless and entranced at the door of Aladdin's chamber during the night, and at Aladdin's command transported the couch, with the bride and bridegroom on it, by the same invisible agency, into the palace of the sultan.

At the instant that the genie had set down the couch with the bride and bridegroom in their own chamber, the sultan came to the door to offer his good wishes to his daughter. The grand minister's son, who was almost perished with cold, by standing in his thin under-garment all night, no sooner heard the knocking at the door than he got out of bed, and ran into the robing-chamber, where he had undressed himself the night before.

The sultan, having opened the door, went to the bed-side, and kissed the princess on the forehead, but was extremely surprised to see her look so melancholy. She only cast at him a sorrowful look, expressive of great affliction. He suspected there was something extraordinary in this silence, and thereupon went immediately to the sultaness's apartment, told her in what a state he found the princess, and how she had received him.

"Sire," said the sultaness, "I will go and see her. She will not receive me in the same manner."

The princess received her mother with sighs and tears, and signs of deep dejection. At last, upon her pressing on her the duty of telling her all her thoughts, she gave to the sultaness a precise description of all that happened to her during the night; on which the sultaness enjoined on her the necessity of silence and discretion, as no one would give credence to so strange a tale. The grand minister's son, elated with the honor of being the sultan's son-in-law, kept silence on his part, and the events of the night were not allowed to cast the least gloom on the festivities on the following day, in continued celebration of the royal marriage.

When night came, the bride and bridegroom were again attended to their chamber with the same ceremonies as on the preceding evening. Aladdin, knowing that this would be so, had already given his commands to the genie of the lamp; and no sooner were they alone than their bed was removed in the same mysterious manner as on the preceding evening; and having passed the night in the same unpleasant way, they were in the morning conveyed to the palace of the sultan. Scarcely had they been replaced in their apartment, when the sultan came to make his compliments to his daughter. The princess could no longer conceal from him the unhappy treatment she had been subjected to, and told him all that had happened, as she had already related it to her mother.

The sultan, on hearing these strange tidings, consulted with the grand minister; and finding from him that his son had been subjected by an invisible agency to even worse treatment, he determined to declare the marriage canceled, and all the festivities, which were yet to last for several days, countermanded and terminated.

This sudden change in the mind of the sultan gave rise to various speculations and reports. Nobody but Aladdin knew the secret, and he kept it with the most scrupulous silence. Neither the sultan nor the grand minister, who had forgotten Aladdin and his request, had the least thought that he had any hand in the strange adventures that befell the bride and bridegroom.

On the very day that the three months contained in the sultan's promise expired, the mother of Aladdin again went to the palace, and stood in the same place in the divan. The sultan knew her again, and directed his minister to have her brought before him.

After having prostrated herself, she made answer, in reply to the sultan: "Sire, I come at the end of three months to ask of you the fulfillment of the promise you made to my son."

The sultan little thought the request of Aladdin's mother was made to him in earnest, or that he would hear any more of the matter. He therefore took counsel with his minister, who suggested that the sultan should attach such conditions to the marriage that no one of the humble condition of Aladdin could possibly fulfill. In accordance with this suggestion of the minister, the sultan replied to the mother of Aladdin: "Good woman, it is true sultans ought to abide by their word, and I am ready to keep mine, by making your son happy in marriage with the princess my daughter. But as I cannot marry her without some further proof of your son being able to support her in royal state, you may tell him I will fulfill my promise as soon as he shall send me forty trays of massy gold, full of the same sort of jewels you have already made me a present of, and carried by the like number of black slaves, who shall be led by as many young and handsome white slaves, all dressed magnificently. On these conditions I am ready to bestow the princess my daughter upon him; therefore, good woman, go and tell him so, and I will wait till you bring me his answer."

Aladdin's mother prostrated herself a second time before the sultan's throne, and retired. On her way home, she laughed within herself at her son's foolish imagination. "Where," said she, "can he get so many large gold trays, and such precious stones to fill them? It is altogether out of his power, and I believe he will not be much pleased with my embassy this time."

When she came home, full of these thoughts, she told Aladdin all the circumstances of her interview with the sultan, and the conditions on which he consented to the marriage. "The sultan expects your answer immediately," said she; and then added, laughing, "I believe he may wait long enough!"

"Not so long, mother, as you imagine," replied Aladdin. "This demand is a mere trifle, and will prove no bar to my marriage with the princess. I will prepare at once to satisfy his request."

The Story of Aladdin

Aladdin retired to his own apartment and summoned the genie of the lamp, and required him to immediately prepare and present the gift, before the sultan closed his morning audience, according to the terms in which it had been prescribed. The genie professed his obedience to the owner of the lamp, and disappeared. Within a very short time, a train of forty black slaves, led by the same number of white slaves, appeared opposite the house in which Aladdin lived. Each black slave carried on his head a basin of massy gold, full of pearls, diamonds, rubies, and emeralds.

Aladdin then addressed his mother: "Madam, pray lose no time; before the sultan and the divan rise, I would have you return to the palace with this present as the dowry demanded for the princess, that he may judge by my diligence and exactness of the ardent and sincere desire I have to procure myself the honor of this alliance."

As soon as this magnificent procession, with Aladdin's mother at its head, had begun to march from Aladdin's house, the whole city was filled with the crowds of people desirous to see so grand a sight. The graceful bearing, elegant form, and wonderful likeness of each slave; their grave walk at an equal distance from each other, the luster of their jeweled girdles, and the brilliancy of the aigrettes of precious stones in their turbans, excited the greatest admiration in the spectators. As they had to pass through several streets to the palace, the whole length of the way was lined with files of spectators. Nothing, indeed, was ever seen so beautiful and brilliant in the sultan's palace, and the richest robes of the emirs of his court were not to be compared to the costly dresses of these slaves, whom they supposed to be kings.

As the sultan, who had been informed of their approach, had given orders for them to be admitted, they met with no obstacle, but went into the divan in regular order, one part turning to the right and the other to the left. After they were all entered, and had formed a semi-circle before the sultan's throne, the black slaves laid the golden trays on the carpet, prostrated themselves, touching the carpet with their foreheads, and at the same time the white slaves did the same. When they rose, the black slaves uncovered the trays, and then all stood with their arms crossed over their breasts.

In the meantime, Aladdin's mother advanced to the foot of the throne, and having prostrated herself, said to the sultan, "Sire, my son knows this present is much below the notice of Princess Buddir al Buddoor; but hopes, nevertheless, that your majesty will accept of it, and make it agreeable to the princess, and with the greater confidence since he has endeavored to conform to the conditions you were pleased to impose."

The sultan, overpowered by the sight of such more than royal magnificence, replied without hesitation to the words of Aladdin's mother: "Go and tell your son that I wait with open arms to embrace him; and the more haste he makes to come and receive the princess my daughter from my hands, the greater pleasure he will do me."

As soon as Aladdin's mother had retired, the sultan put an end to the audience. Rising from his throne, he ordered that the princess's attendants should come and carry the trays into their mistress's apartment, whither he went himself to examine them with her at his leisure. The fourscore slaves were conducted into the palace; and the sultan, telling the princess of their magnificent apparel, ordered them to be brought before her apartment, that she might see through the lattices he had not exaggerated in his account of them.

In the meantime Aladdin's mother reached home, and showed in her air and countenance the good news she brought to her son. "My son," said she, "you may rejoice you are arrived at the height of your desires. The sultan has declared that you shall marry the Princess Buddir al Buddoor. He waits for you with impatience."

Aladdin, enraptured with this news, made his mother very little reply, but retired to his chamber. There he rubbed his lamp, and the obedient genie appeared.

"Genie," said Aladdin, "convey me at once to a bath, and supply me with the richest and most magnificent robe ever worn by a monarch."

No sooner were the words out of his mouth than the genie rendered him, as well as himself, invisible, and transported him into a hummum of the finest marble of all sorts of colors; where he was undressed, without seeing by whom, in a magnificent and spacious hall. He was then well rubbed and washed with various scented waters. After he had passed through several degrees of heat, he came out quite a different man from what he was before. His skin was clear as that of a child, his body lightsome and free; and when he returned into the hall, he found, instead of his own poor raiment, a robe, the magnificence of which astonished him. The genie helped him to dress, and when he had done, transported him back to his own chamber, where he asked him if he had any other commands.

"Yes," answered Aladdin, "bring me a charger that surpasses in beauty and goodness the best in the sultan's stables; with a saddle, bridle, and other caparisons to correspond with his value. Furnish also twenty slaves, as richly clothed as those who carried the present to the sultan, to walk by my side and follow me, and twenty more to go before me in two ranks. Besides these, bring my mother six women slaves to attend her, as richly dressed at least as any of the Princess Buddir al Buddoor's, each carrying a complete dress fit for any sultaness. I want also ten thousand pieces of gold in ten purses; go, and make haste."

As soon as Aladdin had given these orders, the genie disappeared, but presently returned with the horse, the forty slaves, ten of whom carried each a purse containing ten thousand pieces of gold, and six women slaves, each carrying on her head a different dress for Aladdin's mother, wrapped up in a piece of silver tissue, and presented them all to Aladdin.

He presented the six women slaves to his mother, telling her they were her slaves, and that the dresses they had brought were for her use. Of the ten purses Aladdin took four, which he gave to his mother, telling her those were to supply her with necessaries; the other six he left in the hands of the slaves who brought them, with an order to throw them by handfuls among the people as they went to the sultan's palace. The six slaves who carried the purses he ordered likewise to march before him, three on the right hand and three on the left.

When Aladdin had thus prepared himself for his first interview with the sultan, he dismissed the genie, and immediately mounting his charger, began his march, and though he never was on horseback before, appeared with a grace the most experienced horseman might envy. The innumerable concourse of people through whom he passed made the air echo with their acclamations, especially every time the six slaves who carried the purses threw handfuls of gold among the populace.

On Aladdin's arrival at the palace, the sultan was surprised to find him more richly and magnificently robed than he had ever been himself, and was impressed with his good looks and dignity of manner, which were so different from what he expected in the son of one so humble as Aladdin's mother. He embraced him with all the demonstrations of joy, and when he would have fallen at his feet, held him by the hand, and made him sit near his throne. He shortly after led him, amidst the sounds of trumpets, hautboys, and all kinds of music, to a magnificent entertainment, at which the sultan and Aladdin ate by themselves, and the great lords of the court, according to their rank and dignity, sat at different tables.

After the feast, the sultan sent for the chief cadi, and commanded him to draw up a contract of marriage between the Princess Buddir al Buddoor and Aladdin. When the contract had been drawn, the sultan asked Aladdin if he would stay in the palace and complete the ceremonies of the marriage that day.

"Sire," said Aladdin, "though great is my impatience to enter on the honor granted me by your majesty, yet I beg you to permit me first to build a palace worthy to receive the princess your daughter. I pray you to grant me sufficient ground near your palace, and I will have it completed with the utmost expedition."

The sultan granted Aladdin his request, and again embraced him. After which he took his leave with as much politeness as if he had been bred up and had always lived at court.

Aladdin returned home in the order he had come, amidst the acclamations of the people, who wished him all happiness and prosperity. As soon as he dismounted, he retired to his own chamber, took the lamp, and summoned the genie as usual, who professed his allegiance.

"Genie," said Aladdin, "build me a palace fit to receive the Princess Buddir al Buddoor. Let its materials be made of nothing less than porphyry, jasper, agate, lapis lazuli, and the finest marble. Let its walls be massive gold and silver bricks and laid alternately. Let each front contain six windows, and let the lattices of these (except one, which must be left unfinished) be enriched with diamonds, rubies, and emeralds, so that they shall exceed everything of the kind ever seen in the world. Let there be an inner and outer court in front of the palace, and a spacious garden; but above all things, provide a safe treasure house, and fill it with gold and silver. Let there be also kitchens and storehouses, stables full of the finest horses, with their equerries and grooms, and hunting equipage, officers, attendants, and slaves, both men and women, to form a retinue for the princess and myself. Go and execute my wishes."

When Aladdin gave these commands to the genie, the sun was set. The next morning at daybreak the genie presented himself, and, having obtained Aladdin's consent, transported him in a moment to the palace he had made. The genie led him through all the apartments, where he found officers and slaves, habited according to their rank and the services to which they were appointed. The genie then showed him the treasury, which was opened by a treasurer, where Aladdin saw large vases of different sizes, piled up to the top with money, ranged all around the chamber. The genie thence led him to the stables, where were some of the finest horses in the world, and the grooms busy in dressing them; from thence they went to the storehouses, which were filled with all things necessary, both for food and ornament.

When Aladdin had examined every portion of the palace, and particularly the hall with the four-and-twenty windows, and found it far to exceed his fondest expectations, he said, "Genie, there is one thing wanting, a fine carpet for the princess to walk upon from the sultan's palace to mine. Lay one down immediately." The genie disappeared, and Aladdin saw what he desired executed in an instant. The genie then returned, and carried him to his own home.

When the sultan's porters came to open the gates, they were amazed to find what had been an unoccupied garden filled up with a magnificent palace, and a splendid carpet extending to it all the way from the sultan's palace. They told the strange tidings to the grand minister, who informed the sultan.

"It must be Aladdin's palace," the sultan exclaimed, "which I gave him leave to build for my daughter. He has wished to surprise us, and let us see what wonders can be done in only one night."

Aladdin, on his being conveyed by the genie to his own home, requested his mother to go to the Princess Buddir al Buddoor, and tell her that the palace would be ready for her reception in the evening. She went, attended by her women slaves, in the same order as on the preceding day. Shortly after her arrival at the princess's apartment the sultan himself came in, and was surprised to find her, whom he knew only as his suppliant at his divan in humble guise, more richly and sumptuously attired than his own daughter. This gave him a higher opinion of Aladdin, who took such care of his mother, and made her share his wealth and honors.

Shortly after her departure, Aladdin, mounting his horse and attended by his retinue of magnificent attendants, left his paternal home forever, and went to the palace in the same pomp as on the day before. Nor did he forget to take with him the wonderful lamp, to which he owed all his good fortune, nor to wear the ring which was given him as a talisman.

The sultan entertained Aladdin with the utmost magnificence, and at night, on the conclusion of the marriage ceremonies, the princess took leave of the sultan her father. Bands of music led the procession, followed by a hundred state ushers, and the like number of black mutes, in two files, with their officers at their head. Four hundred of the sultan's young pages carried flambeaux on each side, which, together with the illuminations of the sultan's and Aladdin's palaces, made it as light as day. In this order the princess, conveyed in her litter, and accompanied also by Aladdin's mother, carried in a superb litter and attended by her women slaves, proceeded on the carpet which was spread from the sultan's palace to that of Aladdin.

On her arrival Aladdin was ready to receive her at the entrance, and led her into a large hall, illuminated with an infinite number of wax candles, where a noble feast was served up. The dishes were of massy gold, and contained the most delicate viands. The vases, basins, and goblets were gold also, and of exquisite workmanship, and all the other ornaments and embellishments of the hall were answerable to this display. The princess, dazzled to see so much riches collected in one place, said to Aladdin, "I thought, prince, that nothing in the world was so beautiful as the sultan my father's palace, but the sight of this hall alone is sufficient to show I was mistaken."

When the supper was ended, there entered a company of female dancers, who performed, according to the custom of the country, singing at the same time verses in praise of the bride and bridegroom. About midnight Aladdin's mother conducted the bride to the nuptial apartment, and he soon after retired.

The next morning the attendants of Aladdin presented themselves to dress him, and brought him another habit, as rich and magnificent as that worn the day before. He then ordered one of the horses to be got ready, mounted him, and went in the midst of a large troop of slaves to the sultan's palace to entreat him to take a repast in the princess's palace, attended by his grand minister and all the lords of his court. The sultan consented with pleasure, rose up immediately, and, preceded by the principal officers of his palace, and followed by all the great lords of his court, accompanied Aladdin.

The nearer the sultan approached Aladdin's palace, the more he was struck with its beauty; but when he entered it, when he came into the hall and saw the windows, enriched with diamonds, rubies, emeralds, all large perfect stones, he was completely surprised, and said to his son-in-law, "This palace is one of the wonders of the world; for where in all the world besides shall we find walls built of massy gold and silver, and diamonds, rubies, and emeralds composing the windows? But what most surprises me is that a hall of this magnificence should be left with one of its windows incomplete and unfinished."

"Sire," answered Aladdin, "the omission was by design, since I wished that you should have the glory of finishing this hall."

"I take your intention kindly," said the sultan, "and will give orders about it immediately."

After the sultan had finished this magnificent entertainment, provided for him and for his court by Aladdin, he was informed that the jewelers and goldsmiths attended; upon which he returned to the hall, and showed them the window which was unfinished.

"I sent for you," said he, "to fit up this window in as great perfection as the rest. Examine them well, and make all the dispatch you can."

The jewelers and goldsmiths examined the three-and-twenty windows with great attention, and after they had consulted together, to know what each could furnish, they returned, and presented themselves before the sultan, whose principal jeweler, undertaking to speak for the rest, said, "Sire, we are all willing to exert our utmost care and industry to obey you; but among us all we cannot furnish jewels enough for so great a work."

"I have more than are necessary," said the sultan. "Come to my palace, and you shall choose what may answer your purpose."

When the sultan returned to his palace he ordered his jewels to be brought out, and the jewelers took a great quantity, particularly those Aladdin had made him a present of, which they soon used, without making any great advance in their work. They came again several times for more, and in a month's time had not finished half their work. In short, they used all the jewels the sultan had, and borrowed of the minister, but yet the work was not half done.

Aladdin, who knew that all the sultan's endeavors to make this window like the rest were in vain, sent for the jewelers and goldsmiths, and not only commanded them to desist from their work, but ordered them to undo what they had begun, and to carry all their jewels back to the sultan and to the minister. They undid in a few hours what they had been six weeks about, and retired, leaving Aladdin alone in the hall. He took the lamp, which he carried about him, rubbed it, and presently the genie appeared.

"Genie," said Aladdin, "I ordered thee to leave one of the four-and-twenty windows of this hall imperfect, and thou hast executed my commands exactly; now I would have thee make it like the rest."

The genie immediately disappeared. Aladdin went out of the hall, and returning soon after, found the window, as he wished it to be, like the others.

In the meantime the jewelers and goldsmiths repaired to the palace, and were introduced into the sultan's presence, where the chief jeweler presented the precious stones which he had brought back. The sultan asked them if Aladdin had given them any reason for so doing, and they answering that he had given them none, he ordered a horse to be brought, which he mounted, and rode to his son-in-law's palace, with some few attendants on foot, to inquire why he had ordered the completion of the window to be stopped.

Aladdin met him at the gate, and without giving any reply to his inquiries conducted him to the grand saloon, where the sultan, to his great surprise, found that the window, which was left imperfect, corresponded exactly with the others. He fancied at first that he was mistaken, and examined the two windows on each side, and afterward all the four-and-twenty; but when he was convinced that the window which several workmen had been so long about was finished in so short a time, he embraced Aladdin and kissed him between his eyes.

"My son," said he, "what a man you are to do such surprising things always in the twinkling of an eye! There is not your fellow in the world; the more I know, the more I admire you."

The sultan returned to the palace, and after this went frequently to the window to contemplate and admire the wonderful palace of his son-in-law.

Aladdin did not confine himself in his palace, but went with much state, sometimes to one mosque, and sometimes to another, to prayers, or to visit the grand minister or the principal lords of the court. Every time he went out he caused two slaves, who walked by the side of his horse, to throw handfuls of money among the people as he passed through the streets and squares. This generosity gained him the love and blessings of the people, and it was common for them to swear by his head. Thus Aladdin, while he paid all respect to the sultan, won by his affable behavior and liberality the affection of the people.

Aladdin had conducted himself in this manner several years, when the African magician, who had for some years dismissed him from his recollection, determined to inform himself with certainty whether he perished, as he supposed, in the subterranean cave or not. After he had resorted to a long course of magic ceremonies, and had formed a horoscope by which to ascertain Aladdin's fate, what was his surprise to find the appearances to declare that Aladdin, instead of dying in the cave, had made his escape, and was living in royal splendor by the aid of the genie of the wonderful lamp!

On the very next day the magician set out, and traveled with the utmost haste to the capital of China, where, on his arrival, he took up his lodgings in a khan.

He then quickly learned about the wealth, charities, happiness, and splendid palace of Prince Aladdin. Directly he saw the wonderful fabric, he knew that none but the genies, the slaves of the lamp, could have performed such wonders, and, piqued to the quick at Aladdin's high estate, he returned to the khan.

On his return he had recourse to an operation of geomancy to find out where the lamp was--whether Aladdin carried it about with him, or where he left it. The result of his consultation informed him, to his great joy, that the lamp was in the palace.

"Well," said he, rubbing his hands in glee, "I shall have the lamp, and I shall make Aladdin return to his original mean condition."

The next day the magician learned from the chief superintendent of the khan where he lodged that Aladdin had gone on a hunting expedition which was to last for eight days, of which only three had expired. The magician wanted to know no more. He resolved at once on his plans. He went to a coppersmith, and asked for a dozen copper lamps; the master of the shop told him he had not so many by him, but if he would have patience till the next day he would have them ready. The magician appointed his time, and desired him to take care that they should be handsome and well polished.

The next day the magician called for the twelve lamps, paid the man his full price, put them into a basket hanging on his arm, and went directly to Aladdin's palace. As he approached, he began crying, "Who will exchange old lamps for new?" And as he went along, a crowd of children collected, who hooted, and thought him, as did all who chanced to be passing by, a madman or a fool to offer to exchange new lamps for old.

The African magician regarded not their scoffs, hootings, or all they could say to him, but still continued crying, "Who will exchange old lamps for new?" He repeated this so often, walking backward and forward in front of the palace, that the princess, who was then in the hall of the four-and-twenty windows, hearing a man cry something, and seeing a great mob crowding about him, sent one of her women slaves to know what he cried.

The slave returned, laughing so heartily that the princess rebuked her.

"Madam," answered the slave, laughing still, "who can forbear laughing, to see an old man with a basket on his arm, full of fine new lamps, asking to exchange them for old ones? The children and mob, crowding about him so that he can hardly stir, make all the noise they can in derision of him."

Another female slave, hearing this, said, "Now you speak of lamps, I know not whether the princess may have observed it, but there is an old one upon a shelf of the Prince Aladdin's robing room, and whoever owns it will not be sorry to find a new one in its stead. If the princess chooses, she may have the pleasure of trying if this old man is so silly as to give a new lamp for an old one, without taking anything for the exchange."

The Story of Aladdin

The princess, who knew not the value of the lamp and the interest that Aladdin had to keep it safe, entered into the pleasantry and commanded a slave to take it and make the exchange. The slave obeyed, went out of the hall, and no sooner got to the palace gates than he saw the African magician, called to him, and showing him the old lamp, said, "Give me a new lamp for this."

The magician never doubted but this was the lamp he wanted. There could be no other such in this palace, where every utensil was gold or silver. He snatched it eagerly out of the slave's hand, and thrusting it as far as he could into his breast, offered him his basket, and bade him choose which he liked best. The slave picked out one and carried it to the princess; but the change was no sooner made than the place rang with the shouts of the children, deriding the magician's folly.

The African magician stayed no longer near the palace, nor cried anymore, "New lamps for old," but made the best of his way to his khan. His end was answered, and by his silence he got rid of the children and the mob.

As soon as he was out of sight of the two palaces he hastened down the least-frequented streets. Having no more occasion for his lamps or basket, he set all down in a spot where nobody saw him; then going down another street or two, he walked till he came to one of the city gates, and pursuing his way through the suburbs, which were very extensive, at length he reached a lonely spot, where he stopped till the darkness of the night, as the most suitable time for the design he had in contemplation.

When it became quite dark, he pulled the lamp out of his breast and rubbed it. At that summons the genie appeared, and said, "What wouldst thou have? I am ready to obey thee as thy slave, and the slave of all those who have that lamp in their hands; both I and the other slaves of the lamp."

"I command thee," replied the magician, "to transport me immediately, and the palace which thou and the other slaves of the lamp have built in this city, with all the people in it, to Africa."

The genie made no reply, but with the assistance of the other genies, the slaves of the lamp, immediately transported him and the palace, entire, to the spot whither he had been desired to convey it.

Early the next morning when the sultan, according to custom, went to contemplate and admire Aladdin's palace, his amazement was unbounded to find that it could nowhere be seen. He could not comprehend how so large a palace, which he had seen plainly every day for some years, should vanish so soon and not leave the least remains behind. In his perplexity he ordered the grand minister to be sent for with expedition.

The grand minister, who, in secret, bore no good will to Aladdin, intimated his suspicion that the palace was built by magic, and that Aladdin had made his hunting excursion an excuse for the removal of his palace with the same suddenness with which it had been erected. He induced the sultan to send a detachment of his guard, and to have Aladdin seized as a prisoner of state.

On his son-in-law being brought before him, the sultan would not hear a word from him, but ordered him to be put to death.

But the decree caused so much discontent among the people, whose affection Aladdin had secured by his largesses and charities, that the sultan, fearful of an insurrection, was obliged to grant him his life.

When Aladdin found himself at liberty, he again addressed the sultan: "Sire, I pray you to let me know the crime by which I have thus lost the favor of thy countenance."

"Your crime!" answered the sultan. "Wretched man, do you not know it? Follow me, and I will show you."

The sultan then took Aladdin into the apartment from whence he was wont to look at and admire his palace, and said, "You ought to know where your palace stood; look, mind, and tell me what has become of it."

Aladdin did so, and being utterly amazed at the loss of his palace, was speechless. At last recovering himself, he said, "It is true, I do not see the palace. It is vanished; but I had no concern in its removal. I beg you to give me forty days, and if in that time I cannot restore it, I will offer my head to be disposed of at your pleasure."

"I give you the time you ask, but at the end of the forty days forget not to present yourself before me."

Aladdin went out of the sultan's palace in a condition of exceeding humiliation. The lords who had courted him in the days of his splendor now declined to have any communication with him. For three days he wandered about the city, exciting the wonder and compassion of the multitude by asking everybody he met if they had seen his palace, or could tell him anything of it.

On the third day he wandered into the country, and as he was approaching a river he fell down the bank with so much violence that he rubbed the ring which the magician had given him so hard, by holding on to the rock to save himself, that immediately the same genie appeared whom he had seen in the cave where the magician had left him.

"What wouldst thou have?" said the genie. "I am ready to obey thee as thy slave, and the slave of all those that have that ring on their finger; both I and the other slaves of the ring."

Aladdin, agreeably surprised at an offer of help so little expected, replied, "Genie, show me where the palace I caused to be built now stands, or transport it back where it first stood."

"Your command," answered the genie, "is not wholly in my power; I am only the slave of the ring, and not of the lamp."

"I command thee, then," replied Aladdin, "by the power of the ring, to transport me to the spot where my palace stands, in whatever part of the world it may be."

These words were no sooner out of his mouth than the genie transported him into Africa, to the midst of a large plain, where his palace stood at no great distance from a city, and, placing him exactly under the window of the princess's apartment, left him.

Now it so happened that shortly after Aladdin had been transported by the slave of the ring to the neighborhood of his palace, that one of the attendants of the Princess Buddir al Buddoor, looking through the window, perceived him and instantly told her mistress. The princess, who could not believe the joyful tidings, hastened herself to the window, and seeing Aladdin, immediately opened it. The noise of opening the window made Aladdin turn his head that way, and perceiving the princess, he saluted her with an air that expressed his joy.

"To lose no time," said she to him, "I have sent to have the private door opened for you; enter, and come up."

The private door, which was just under the princess's apartment, was soon opened, and Aladdin was conducted up into the chamber. It is impossible to express the joy of both at seeing each other, after so cruel a separation. After embracing and shedding tears of joy, they sat down, and Aladdin said, "I beg of you, princess, to tell me what is become of an old lamp which stood upon a shelf in my dressing chamber."

"Alas!" answered the princess, "I was afraid our misfortune might be owing to that lamp; and what grieves me most is that I have been the cause of it. I was foolish enough to exchange the old lamp for a new one, and the next morning I found myself in this unknown country, which I am told is Africa."

"Princess," said Aladdin, interrupting her, "you have explained all by telling me we are in Africa. I desire you only to tell me if you know where the old lamp now is."

"The African magician carries it carefully wrapped up in his bosom," said the princess; "and this I can assure you, because he pulled it out before me, and showed it to me in triumph."

"Princess," said Aladdin, "I think I have found the means to deliver you and to regain possession of the lamp, on which all my prosperity depends. To execute this design, it is necessary

49

for me to go to the town. I shall return by noon, and will then tell you what must be done by you to insure success. In the meantime, I shall disguise myself, and I beg that the private door may be opened at the first knock."

When Aladdin was out of the palace, he looked round him on all sides, and perceiving a peasant going into the country, hastened after him. When he had overtaken him, he made a proposal to him to change clothes, which the man agreed to. When they had made the exchange, the countryman went about his business, and Aladdin entered the neighboring city. After traversing several streets, he came to that part of the town where the merchants and artisans had their particular streets according to their trades. He went into that of the druggists; and entering one of the largest and best furnished shops, asked the druggist if he had a certain powder, which he named.

The druggist, judging Aladdin by his habit to be very poor, told him he had it, but that it was very dear; upon which Aladdin, penetrating his thoughts, pulled out his purse, and showing him some gold, asked for half a dram of the powder, which the druggist weighed and gave him, telling him the price was a piece of gold. Aladdin put the money into his hand, and hastened to the palace, which he entered at once by the private door.

When he came into the princess's apartment he said to her, "Princess, you must take your part in the scheme which I propose for our deliverance. You must overcome your aversion for the magician, and assume a most friendly manner toward him, and ask him to oblige you by partaking of an entertainment in your apartments. Before he leaves, ask him to exchange cups with you, which he, gratified at the honor you do him, will gladly do, when you must give him the cup containing this powder. On drinking it he will instantly fall asleep, and we will obtain the lamp, whose slaves will do all our bidding, and restore us and the palace to the capital of China."

The princess obeyed to the utmost her husband's instructions. She assumed a look of pleasure on the next visit of the magician, and asked him to an entertainment, which he most willingly accepted. At the close of the evening, during which the princess had tried all she could to please him, she asked him to exchange cups with her, and giving the signal, had the drugged cup brought to her, which she gave to the magician. Out of compliment to the princess he drank it to the very last drop, when he fell back lifeless on the sofa.

The princess, in anticipation of the success of her scheme, had so placed her women from the great hall to the foot of the staircase that the word was no sooner given that the African magician was fallen backward, than the door was opened, and Aladdin admitted to the hall. The princess rose from her seat, and ran, overjoyed, to embrace him; but he stopped her, and said, "Princess, retire to your apartment; and let me be left alone, while I endeavor to transport you back to China as speedily as you were brought from thence."

When the princess, her women, and slaves were gone out of the hall, Aladdin shut the door, and going directly to the dead body of the magician, opened his vest, took out the lamp, which was carefully wrapped up, and rubbing it, the genie immediately appeared.

"Genie," said Aladdin, "I command thee to transport this palace instantly to the place from whence it was brought hither."

The genie bowed his head in token of obedience, and disappeared. Immediately the palace was transported into China, and its removal was felt only by two little shocks, the one when it was lifted up, the other when it was set down, and both in a very short interval of time.

On the morning after the restoration of Aladdin's palace the sultan was looking out of his window, mourning over the fate of his daughter, when he thought that he saw the vacancy created by the disappearance of the palace to be again filled up.

On looking more attentively, he was convinced beyond the power of doubt that it was his son-in-law's palace. Joy and gladness succeeded to sorrow and grief. He at once ordered a horse to be saddled, which he mounted that instant, thinking he could not make haste enough to the place.

Aladdin rose that morning by daybreak, put on one of the most magnificent habits his wardrobe afforded, and went up into the hall of the twenty-four windows, from whence he perceived the sultan approaching, and received him at the foot of the great staircase, helping him to dismount.

He led the sultan into the princess's apartment. The happy father embraced her with tears of joy; and the princess, on her side, afforded similar testimonies of her extreme pleasure. After a short interval, devoted to mutual explanations of all that had happened, the sultan restored Aladdin to his favor, and expressed his regret for the apparent harshness with which he had treated him.

"My son," said he, "be not displeased at my proceedings against you; they arose from my paternal love, and therefore you ought to forgive the excesses to which it hurried me."

"Sire," replied Aladdin, "I have not the least reason to complain of your conduct, since you did nothing but what your duty required. This infamous magician, the basest of men, was the sole cause of my misfortune."

The African magician, who was thus twice foiled in his endeavor to rain Aladdin, had a younger brother, who was as skillful a magician as himself and exceeded him in wickedness and hatred of mankind. By mutual agreement they communicated with each other once a year, however widely separate might be their place of residence from each other. The younger brother, not having received as usual his annual communication, prepared to take a horoscope and ascertain his brother's proceedings. He, as well as his brother, always carried a geomantic square instrument about him; he prepared the sand, cast the points, and drew the figures. On examining the planetary crystal, he found that his brother was no longer living, but had been poisoned; and by another observation, that he was in the capital of the kingdom of China; also, that the person who had poisoned him was of mean birth, though married to a princess, a sultan's daughter.

When the magician had informed himself of his brother's fate he resolved immediately to avenge his death, and at once departed for China; where, after crossing plains, rivers, mountains, deserts, and a long tract of country without delay, he arrived after incredible fatigues. When he came to the capital of China he took a lodging at a khan. His magic art soon revealed to him that Aladdin was the person who had been the cause of the death of his brother. He had heard, too, all the persons of repute in the city talking of a woman called Fatima, who was retired from the world, and of the miracles she wrought. As he fancied that this woman might be serviceable to him in the project he had conceived, he made more minute inquiries, and requested to be informed more particularly who that holy woman was, and what sort of miracles she performed.

"What!" said the person whom he addressed, "have you never seen or heard of her? She is the admiration of the whole town, for her fasting, her austerities, and her exemplary life. Except Mondays and Fridays, she never stirs out of her little cell; and on those days on which she comes into the town she does an infinite deal of good; for there is not a person who is diseased but she puts her hand on him and cures him."

Having ascertained the place where the hermitage of this holy woman was, the magician went at night, and plunged a poniard into her heart--killed this good woman. In the morning he dyed his face of the same hue as hers, and arraying himself in her garb, taking her veil, the large necklace she wore round her waist, and her stick, went straight to the palace of Aladdin.

As soon as the people saw the holy woman, as they imagined him to be, they presently gathered about him in a great crowd. Some begged his blessing, others kissed his hand, and others, more reserved, kissed only the hem of his garment; while others, suffering from disease, stooped for him to lay his hands upon them; which he did, muttering some words in form of prayer, and, in short, counterfeiting so well that everybody took him for the holy woman. He came at last to the square before Aladdin's palace. The crowd and the noise were so great that the princess, who was in the hall of the four-and-twenty windows, heard it, and asked what was the matter. One of her women told her it

54

was a great crowd of people collected about the holy woman to be cured of diseases by the imposition of her hands.

The princess, who had long heard of this holy woman, but had never seen her, was very desirous to have some conversation with her. The chief officer perceiving this, told her it was an easy matter to bring the woman to her if she desired and commanded it; and the princess expressing her wishes, he immediately sent four slaves for the pretended holy woman.

As soon as the crowd saw the attendants from the palace, they made way; and the magician, perceiving also that they were coming for him, advanced to meet them, overjoyed to find his plot succeed so well.

"Holy woman," said one of the slaves, "the princess wishes to see you, and has sent us for you."

"The princess does me too great an honor," replied the false Fatima; "I am ready to obey her command." And at the same time he followed the slaves to the palace.

When the pretended Fatima had made his obeisance, the princess said, "My good mother, I have one thing to request, which you must not refuse me; it is, to stay with me, that you may edify me with your way of living, and that I may learn from your good example."

"Princess," said the counterfeit Fatima, "I beg of you not to ask what I cannot consent to without neglecting my prayers and devotion."

"That shall be no hindrance to you," answered the princess; "I have a great many apartments unoccupied; you shall choose which you like best, and have as much liberty to perform your devotions as if you were in your own cell."

The magician, who really desired nothing more than to introduce himself into the palace, where it would be a much easier matter for him to execute his designs, did not long excuse himself from accepting the obliging offer which the princess made him.

"Princess," said he, "whatever resolution a poor wretched woman as I am may have made to renounce the pomp and grandeur of this world, I dare not presume to oppose the will and commands of so pious and charitable a princess."

Upon this the princess, rising up, said, "Come with me. I will show you what vacant apartments I have, that you may make choice of that you like best." The magician followed the princess, and of all the apartments she showed him, made choice of that which was the worst, saying that was too good for him, and that he only accepted it to please her.

Afterward the princess would have brought him back again into the great hall to make him dine with her; but he, considering that he should then be obliged to show his face, which he had always taken care to conceal with Fatima's veil, and fearing that the princess would find out that he was not Fatima, begged of her earnestly to excuse him, telling her that he never ate anything but bread and dried fruits, and desiring to eat that slight repast in his own apartment.

The princess granted his request, saying, "You may be as free here, good mother, as if you were in your own cell: I will order you a dinner, but remember, I expect you as soon as you have finished your repast."

After the princess had dined, and the false Fatima had been sent for by one of the attendants, he again waited upon her. "My good mother," said the princess, "I am overjoyed to see so holy a woman as yourself, who will confer a blessing upon this palace. But now I am speaking of the palace, pray how do you like it? And before I show it all to you, tell me first what you think of this hall."

Upon this question, the counterfeit Fatima surveyed the hall from one end to the other. When he had examined it well, he said to the princess, "As far as such a solitary being as I am, who am unacquainted with what the world calls beautiful, can judge, this hall is truly admirable; there wants but one thing."

"What is that, good mother?" demanded the princess; "tell me, I conjure you. For my part, I always believed, and have heard say, it wanted nothing; but if it does, it shall be supplied."

"Princess," said the false Fatima, with great dis-simulation, "forgive me the liberty I have taken; but my opinion is, if it can be of any importance, that if a roc's egg were hung up in the middle of the dome, this hall would have no parallel in the four quarters of the world, and your palace would be the wonder of the universe."

"My good mother," said the princess, "what is a roc, and where may one get an egg?"

"Princess," replied the pretended Fatima, "it is a bird of prodigious size, which inhabits the summit of Mount Caucasus; the architect who built your palace can get you one."

After the princess had thanked the false Fatima for what she believed her good advice, she conversed with her upon other matters; but she could not forget the roc's egg, which she resolved to request of Aladdin when next he should visit his apartments. He did so in the course of that evening, and shortly after he entered, the princess thus addressed him: "I always believed that our palace was the most superb, magnificent, and complete in the world: but I will tell you now what it wants, and that is a roc's egg hung up in the midst of the dome."

"Princess," replied Aladdin, "it is enough that you think it wants such an ornament; you shall see by the diligence which I use in obtaining it, that there is nothing which I would not do for your sake."

Aladdin left the Princess Buddir al Buddoor that moment, and went up into the hall of four-and-twenty windows, where, pulling out of his bosom the lamp, which after the danger he had been exposed to he always carried about him, he rubbed it; upon which the genie immediately appeared.

"Genie," said Aladdin, "I command thee, in the name of this lamp, bring a roc's egg to be hung up in the middle of the dome of the hall of the palace."

Aladdin had no sooner pronounced these words than the hall shook as if ready to fall; and the genie said, in a loud and terrible voice, "Is it not enough that I and the other slaves of the lamp have done everything for you, but you, by an unheard-of ingratitude, must command me to bring my master, and hang him up in the midst of this dome? This attempt deserves that you, the princess, and the palace should be immediately reduced to ashes; but you are spared because this request does not come from yourself. Its true author is the brother of the African magician, your enemy whom you have destroyed. He is now in your palace, disguised in the habit of the holy woman Fatima, whom he has murdered; at his suggestion your wife makes this pernicious demand. His design is to kill you; therefore take care of yourself." After these words the genie disappeared.

Aladdin resolved at once what to do. He returned to the princess's apartment, and without mentioning a word of what had happened, sat down, and complained of a great pain which had suddenly seized his head. On hearing this, the princess told him how she had invited the holy Fatima to stay with her, and that she was now in the palace; and at the request of the prince, ordered her to be summoned to her at once.

When the pretended Fatima came, Aladdin said, "Come hither, good mother; I am glad to see you here at so fortunate a time. I am tormented with a violent pain in my head, and request your assistance, and hope you will not refuse me that cure which you impart to afflicted persons."

So saying, he arose, but held down his head. The counterfeit Fatima advanced toward him, with his hand all the time on a dagger concealed in his girdle under his gown. Observing this, Aladdin snatched the weapon from his hand, pierced him to the heart with his own dagger, and then pushed him down on the floor.

"My dear prince, what have you done?" cried the princess, in surprise. "You have killed the holy woman!"

"No, my princess," answered Aladdin, with emotion, "I have not killed Fatima, but a villain who would have assassinated me, if I had not prevented him. This wicked man," added he, uncovering his face, "is the brother of the magician who attempted our ruin. He has strangled the true Fatima, and disguised himself in her clothes with intent to murder me."

Aladdin then informed her how the genie had told him these facts, and how narrowly she and the palace had escaped destruction though his treacherous suggestion which had led to her request.

Thus was Aladdin delivered from the persecution of the two brothers, who were magicians. Within a few years the sultan died in a good old age, and as he left no male children, the Princess Buddir al Buddoor succeeded him, and she and Aladdin reigned together many years, and left a numerous and illustrious posterity.

The History of Ali Baba
And the Forty Thieves

There once lived in a town of Persia two brothers, one named Cassim and the other Ali Baba. Their father divided a small inheritance equally between them. Cassim married a very rich wife, and became a wealthy merchant. Ali Baba married a woman as poor as himself, and lived by cutting wood, and bringing it upon three asses into the town to sell.

One day, when Ali Baba was in the forest and had just cut wood enough to load his asses, he saw at a distance a great cloud of dust, which seemed to approach him. He observed it with attention, and distinguished soon after a body of horsemen, whom he suspected might be robbers. He determined to leave his asses to save himself. He climbed up a large tree, planted on a high rock, whose branches were thick enough to conceal him, and yet enabled him to see all that passed without being discovered.

The troop, who were to the number of forty, all well mounted and armed, came to the foot of the rock on which the tree stood, and there dismounted. Every man unbridled his horse, tied him to some shrub, and hung about his neck a bag of corn which they had brought behind them. Then each of them took off his saddle-bag, which seemed to Ali Baba from its weight to be full of gold and silver. One, whom he took to be their captain, came under the tree in which Ali Baba was concealed; and making his way through some shrubs, pronounced these words: "Open, Sesame!" As soon as the captain of the robbers had thus spoken, a door opened in the rock; and after he had made all his troop enter before him, he followed them, when the door shut again of itself.

61

The robbers stayed some time within the rock, during which Ali Baba, fearful of being caught, remained in the tree.

At last the door opened again, and as the captain went in last, so he came out first, and stood to see them all pass by him; when Ali Baba heard him make the door close by pronouncing these words, "Shut, Sesame!" Every man at once went and bridled his horse, fastened his wallet, and mounted again. When the captain saw them all ready, he put himself at their head, and they returned the way they had come.

Ali Baba followed them with his eyes as far as he could see them; and afterward stayed a considerable time before he descended. Remembering the words the captain of the robbers used to cause the door to open and shut, he had the curiosity to try if his pronouncing them would have the same effect. Accordingly, he went among the shrubs, and perceiving the door concealed behind them, stood before it, and said, "Open, Sesame!" The door instantly flew wide open.

Ali Baba, who expected a dark, dismal cavern, was surprised to see a well-lighted and spacious chamber, which received the light from an opening at the top of the rock, and in which were all sorts of provisions, rich bales of silk, stuff, brocade, and valuable carpeting, piled upon one another, gold and silver ingots in great heaps, and money in bags. The sight of all these riches made him suppose that this cave must have been occupied for ages by robbers, who had succeeded one another.

Ali Baba went boldly into the cave, and collected as much of the gold coin, which was in bags, as he thought his three asses could carry. When he had loaded them with the bags, he laid wood over them in such a manner that they could not be seen. When he had passed in and out as often as he wished, he stood before the door, and pronouncing the words, "Shut, Sesame!" the door closed of itself. He then made the best of his way to town.

When Ali Baba got home he drove his asses into a little yard, shut the gates very carefully, threw off the wood that covered the panniers, carried the bags into his house, and ranged them in order before his wife. He then emptied the bags, which raised such a great heap of gold as dazzled his wife's eyes, and then he told her the whole adventure from beginning to end, and, above all, recommended her to keep it secret.

The wife rejoiced greatly at their good fortune, and would count all the gold piece by piece.

"Wife," replied Ali Baba, "you do not know what you undertake, when you pretend to count the money; you will never have done. I will dig a hole, and bury it. There is no time to be lost."

"You are in the right, husband," replied she, "but let us know, as nigh as possible, how much we have. I will borrow a small measure, and measure it, while you dig the hole."

Away the wife ran to her brother-in-law Cassim, who lived just by, and addressing herself to his wife, desired that she lend her a measure for a little while. Her sister-in-law asked her whether she would have a great or a small one. The other asked for a small one. She bade her stay a little, and she would readily fetch one.

The sister-in-law did so, but as she knew Ali Baba's poverty, she was curious to know what sort of grain his wife wanted to measure, and artfully putting some suet at the bottom of the measure, brought it to her, with an excuse that she was sorry that she had made her stay so long, but that she could not find it sooner.

Ali Baba's wife went home, set the measure upon the heap of gold, filled it, and emptied it often upon the sofa, till she had done, when she was very well satisfied to find the number of measures amounted to so many as they did, and went to tell her husband, who had almost finished digging the hole. When Ali Baba was burying the gold, his wife, to show her exactness and diligence to her sister-in-law, carried the measure back again, but without taking notice that a piece of gold had stuck to the bottom.

"Sister," said she, giving it to her again, "you see that I have not kept your measure long. I am obliged to you for it, and return it with thanks."

As soon as Ali Baba's wife was gone, Cassim's looked at the bottom of the measure, and was in inexpressible surprise to find a piece of gold sticking to it. Envy immediately possessed her breast.

"What!" said she, "has Ali Baba gold so plentiful as to measure it? Whence has he all this wealth?"

Cassim, her husband, was at his counting house. When he came home his wife said to him, "Cassim, I know you think yourself rich, but Ali Baba is infinitely richer than you. He does not count his money, but measures it."

Cassim desired her to explain the riddle, which she did, by telling him the stratagem she had used to make the discovery, and showed him the piece of money, which was so old that they could not tell in what prince's reign it was coined.

Cassim, after he had married the rich widow, had never treated Ali Baba as a brother, but neglected him; and now, instead of being pleased, he conceived a base envy at his brother's prosperity. He could not sleep all that night, and went to him in the morning before sunrise.

"Ali Baba," said he, "I am surprised at you. You pretend to be miserably poor, and yet you measure gold. My wife found this at the bottom of the measure you borrowed yesterday."

By this discourse, Ali Baba perceived that Cassim and his wife, through his own wife's folly, knew what they had so much reason to conceal; but what was done could not be undone. Therefore, without showing the least surprise or trouble, he confessed all, and offered his brother part of his treasure to keep the secret.

"I expect as much," replied Cassim haughtily; "but I must know exactly where this treasure is, and how I may visit it myself when I choose. Otherwise I will go and inform against you, and then you will not only get no more, but will lose all you have, and I shall have a share for my information."

Ali Baba told him all he desired, even to the very words he was to use to gain admission into the cave.

Cassim rose the next morning long before the sun, and set out for the forest with ten mules bearing great chests, which he designed to fill, and followed the road which Ali Baba had pointed out to him. He was not long before he reached the rock, and found out the place, by the tree and other marks which his brother had given him. When he reached the entrance of the cavern, he pronounced the words, "Open, Sesame!" The door immediately opened, and, when he was in, closed upon him. In examining the cave, he was in great admiration to find much more riches than he had expected from Ali Baba's relation. He quickly laid as many bags of gold as he could carry at the door of the cavern; but his thoughts were so full of the great riches he should possess that he could not think of the necessary word to make it open, but instead of "Sesame," said, "Open, Barley!" and was much amazed to find that the door remained fast shut. He named several sorts of grain, but still the door would not open.

Cassim had never expected such an incident, and was so alarmed at the danger he was in, that the more he endeavored to remember the word "Sesame," the more his memory was confounded, and he had as much forgotten it as if he had never heard it mentioned. He threw down the bags he had loaded himself with, and walked distractedly up and down the cave, without having the least regard to the riches that were around him.

About noon the robbers visited their cave. At some distance they saw Cassim's mules straggling about the rock, with great chests on their backs. Alarmed at this, they galloped full speed to the cave. They drove away the mules, who strayed through the forest so far that they were soon out of sight, and went directly, with their naked sabers in their hands, to the door, which, on their captain pronouncing the proper words, immediately opened.

Cassim, who heard the noise of the horses' feet, at once guessed the arrival of the robbers, and resolved to make one effort for his life. He rushed to the door, and no sooner saw the door open, than he ran out and threw the leader down, but could not escape the other robbers, who with their scimitars soon deprived him of life.

The first care of the robbers after this was to examine the cave. They found all the bags which Cassim had brought to the door, to be ready to load his mules, and carried them again to their places, but they did not miss what Ali Baba had taken away before. Then holding a council, and deliberating upon this occurrence, they guessed that Cassim, when he was in, could not get out again, but could not imagine how he had learned the secret words by which alone he could enter. They could not deny the fact of his being there; and to terrify any person or accomplice who should attempt the same thing, they agreed to cut Cassim's body into four quarters--to hang two on one side, and two on the other, within the door of the cave. They had no sooner taken this resolution than they put it in execution; and when they had nothing more to detain them, left the place of their hoards well closed. They mounted their horses, went to beat the roads again, and to attack the caravans they might meet.

In the meantime, Cassim's wife was very uneasy when night came, and her husband was not returned. She ran to Ali Baba in great alarm, and said, "I believe, brother-in-law, that you know Cassim is gone to the forest, and upon what account. It is now night, and he has not returned. I am afraid some misfortune has happened to him."

Ali Baba told her that she need not frighten herself, for that certainly Cassim would not think it proper to come into the town till the night should be pretty far advanced.

Cassim's wife, considering how much it concerned her husband to keep the business secret, was the more easily persuaded to believe her brother-in-law. She went home again, and waited patiently till midnight. Then her fear redoubled, and her grief was the more sensible because she was forced to keep it to herself. She repented of her foolish curiosity, and cursed her desire of prying into the affairs of her brother and sister-in-law. She spent all the night in weeping; and as soon as it was day went to them, telling them, by her tears, the cause of her coming.

Ali Baba did not wait for his sister-in-law to desire him to go to see what was become of Cassim, but departed immediately with his three asses, begging of her first to moderate her grief. He went to the forest, and when he came near the rock, having seen neither his brother nor his mules on his way, was seriously alarmed at finding some blood spilt near the door, which he took for an ill omen; but when he had pronounced the word, and the door had opened, he was struck with horror at the dismal sight of his brother's body. He was not long in determining how he should pay the last dues to his brother; but without adverting to the little fraternal affection he had shown for him, went into the cave, to find something to enshroud his remains. Having loaded one of his asses with them, he covered them over with wood. The other two asses he loaded with bags of gold, covering them with wood also as before; and then, bidding the door shut, he came away; but was so cautious as to stop some time at the end of the forest, that he might not go into the town before night. When he came home he drove the two asses loaded with gold into his little yard, and left the care of unloading them to his wife, while he led the other to his sister-in-law's house.

Ali Baba knocked at the door, which was opened by Morgiana, a clever, intelligent slave, who was fruitful in inventions to meet the most difficult circumstances. When he came into the court he unloaded the ass, and taking Morgiana aside, said to her, "You must observe an inviolable secrecy. Your master's body is contained in these two panniers. We must bury him as if he had died a natural death. Go now and tell your mistress. I leave the matter to your wit and skillful devices."

Ali Baba helped to place the body in Cassim's house, again recommended to Morgiana to act her part well, and then returned with his ass.

Morgiana went out early the next morning to a druggist and asked for a sort of lozenge which was considered efficacious in the most dangerous disorders. The apothecary inquired who was ill. She replied, with a sigh, her good master Cassim himself; and that he could neither eat nor speak.

In the evening Morgiana went to the same druggist again, and with tears in her eyes, asked for an essence which they used to give to sick people only when in the last extremity.

"Alas!" said she, taking it from the apothecary, "I am afraid that this remedy will have no better effect than the lozenges; and that I shall lose my good master."

On the other hand, as Ali Baba and his wife were often seen to go between Cassim's and their own house all that day, and to seem melancholy, nobody was surprised in the evening to hear the lamentable shrieks and cries of Cassim's wife and Morgiana, who gave out everywhere that her master was dead. The next morning at daybreak, Morgiana went to an old cobbler whom she knew to be always ready at his stall, and bidding him good morrow, put a piece of gold into his hand, saying, "Baba Mustapha, you must bring with you your sewing tackle, and come with me; but I must tell you, I shall blindfold you when you come to such a place."

Baba Mustapha seemed to hesitate a little at these words. "Oh! oh!" replied he, "you would have me do something against my conscience, or against my honor?"

"God forbid," said Morgiana, putting another piece of gold into his hand, "that I should ask anything that is contrary to your honor! Only come along with me, and fear nothing."

Baba Mustapha went with Morgiana, who, after she had bound his eyes with a handkerchief at the place she had mentioned, conveyed him to her deceased master's house, and never unloosed his eyes till he had entered the room where she had put the corpse together. "Baba Mustapha," said she, "you must make haste and sew the parts of this body together; and when you have done, I will give you another piece of gold."

After Baba Mustapha had finished his task, she blindfolded him again, gave him the third piece of gold as she had promised, and recommending secrecy to him, carried him back to the place where she first bound his eyes, pulled off the bandage, and let him go home, but watched him that he returned toward his stall, till he was quite out of sight, for fear he should have the curiosity to return and dodge her; she then went home.

Morgiana, on her return, warmed some water to wash the body, and at the same time Ali Baba perfumed it with incense, and wrapped it in the burying clothes with the accustomed ceremonies. Not long after the proper officer brought the bier, and when the attendants of the mosque, whose business it was to wash the dead, offered to perform their duty, she told them it was done already. Shortly after this the imaun and the other ministers of the mosque arrived. Four neighbors carried the corpse to the burying-ground, following the imaun, who recited some prayers. Ali Baba came after with some neighbors, who often relieved the others in carrying the bier to the burying-ground. Morgiana, a slave to the deceased, followed in the procession, weeping, beating her breast, and tearing her hair. Cassim's wife stayed at home mourning, uttering lamentable cries with the women of the neighborhood, who came, according to custom, during the funeral, and joining their lamentations with hers filled the quarter far and near with sounds of sorrow.

In this manner Cassim's melancholy death was concealed and hushed up between Ali Baba, his widow, and Morgiana his slave, with so much contrivance that nobody in the city had the least knowledge or suspicion of the cause of it. Three or four days after the funeral, Ali Baba removed his few goods openly to his sister's house, in which it was agreed that he should in future live; but the money he had taken from the robbers he conveyed thither by night. As for Cassim's warehouse, he intrusted it entirely to the management of his eldest son.

While these things were being done, the forty robbers again visited their retreat in the forest. Great, then, was their surprise to find Cassim's body taken away, with some of their bags of gold. "We are certainly discovered," said the captain. "The removal of the body and the loss of some of our money, plainly shows that the man whom we killed had an accomplice: and for our own lives' sake we must try to find him. What say you, my lads?"

All the robbers unanimously approved of the captain's proposal.

"Well," said the captain, "one of you, the boldest and most skillful among you, must go into the town, disguised as a traveler and a stranger, to try if he can hear any talk of the man whom we have killed, and endeavor to find out who he was, and where he lived. This is a matter of the first importance, and for fear of any treachery I propose that whoever undertakes this business without success, even though the failure arises only from an error of judgment, shall suffer death."

Without waiting for the sentiments of his companions, one of the robbers started up, and said, "I submit to this condition, and think it an honor to expose my life to serve the troop."

After this robber had received great commendations from the captain and his comrades, he disguised himself so that nobody would take him for what he was; and taking his leave of the troop that night, he went into the town just at daybreak. He walked up and down, till accidentally he came to Baba Mustapha's stall, which was always open before any of the shops.

Baba Mustapha was seated with an awl in his hand, just going to work. The robber saluted him, bidding him good morrow; and perceiving that he was old, said, "Honest man, you begin to work very early; is it possible that one of your age can see so well? I question, even if it were somewhat lighter, whether you could see to stitch."

"You do not know me," replied Baba Mustapha; "for old as I am, I have extraordinary good eyes; and you will not doubt it when I tell you that I sewed the body of a dead man together in a place where I had not so much light as I have now."

"A dead body!" exclaimed the robber, with affected amazement.

"Yes, yes," answered Baba Mustapha. "I see you want me to speak out, but you shall know no more."

The robber felt sure that he had discovered what he sought. He pulled out a piece of gold, and putting it into Baba Mustapha's hand, said to him, "I do not want to learn your secret, though I can assure you you might safely trust me with it. The only thing I desire of you is to show me the house where you stitched up the dead body."

"If I were disposed to do you that favor," replied Baba Mustapha, "I assure you I cannot. I was taken to a certain place, whence I was led blindfold to the house, and afterward brought back in the same manner. You see, therefore, the impossibility of my doing what you desire."

"Well," replied the robber, "you may, however, remember a little of the way that you were led blindfold. Come, let me blind your eyes at the same place. We will walk together; perhaps you may recognize some part, and as every one should be paid for his trouble here is another piece of gold for you; gratify me in what I ask you." So saying, he put another piece of gold into his hand.

The two pieces of gold were great temptations to Baba Mustapha. He looked at them a long time in his hand, without saying a word, but at last he pulled out his purse and put them in.

"I cannot promise," said he to the robber, "that I can remember the way exactly; but since you desire, I will try what I can do."

At these words Baba Mustapha rose up, to the great joy of the robber, and led him to the place where Morgiana had bound his eyes.

"It was here," said Baba Mustapha, "I was blindfolded; and I turned this way."

The robber tied his handkerchief over his eyes, and walked by him till he stopped directly at Cassim's house, where Ali Baba then lived. The thief, before he pulled off the band, marked the door with a piece of chalk, which he had ready in his hand, and then asked him if he knew whose house that was; to which Baba Mustapha replied that as he did not live in that neighborhood, he could not tell.

The robber, finding that he could discover no more from Baba Mustapha, thanked him for the trouble he had taken, and left him to go back to his stall, while he returned to the forest, persuaded that he should be very well received.

A little after the robber and Baba Mustapha had parted, Morgiana went out of Ali Baba's house upon some errand, and upon her return, seeing the mark the robber had made, stopped to observe it.

"What can be the meaning of this mark?" said she to herself. "Somebody intends my master no good. However, with whatever intention it was done, it is advisable to guard against the worst."

Accordingly, she fetched a piece of chalk, and marked two or three doors on each side in the same manner, without saying a word to her master or mistress.

In the meantime the robber rejoined his troop in the forest, and recounted to them his success, expatiating upon his good fortune in meeting so soon with the only person who could inform him of what he wanted to know. All the robbers listened to him with the utmost satisfaction. Then the captain, after commending his diligence, addressing himself to them all, said, "Comrades, we have no time to lose. Let us set off well armed, without its appearing who we are; but that we may not excite any suspicion, let only one or two go into the town together, and join at our rendezvous, which shall be the great square. In the meantime, our comrade who brought us the good news and I will go and find out the house, that we may consult what had best be done."

This speech and plan was approved of by all, and they were soon ready. They filed off in parties of two each, after some interval of time, and got into the town without being in the least suspected. The captain, and he who had visited the town in the morning as spy, came in the last. He led the captain into the street where he had marked Ali Baba's residence; and when they came to the first of the houses which Morgiana had marked, he pointed it out. But the captain observed that the next door was chalked in the same manner, and in the same place; and showing it to his guide, asked him which house it was, that, or the first. The guide was so confounded, that he knew not what answer to make; but he was still more puzzled when he and the captain saw five or six houses similarly marked. He assured the captain, with an oath, that he had marked but one, and could not tell who had chalked the rest, so that he could not distinguish the house which the cobbler had stopped at.

The captain, finding that their design had proved abortive, went directly to their place of rendezvous, and told his troop that they had lost their labor, and must return to their cave. He himself set them the example, and they all returned as they had come.

When the troop was all got together, the captain told them the reason of their returning; and presently the conductor was declared by all worthy of death. He condemned himself, acknowledging that he ought to have taken better precaution, and prepared to receive the stroke from him who was appointed to cut off his head.

But as the safety of the troop required the discovery of the second intruder into the cave, another of the gang, who promised himself that he should succeed better, presented himself, and his offer being accepted he went and corrupted Baba Mustapha as the other had done; and being shown the house, marked it in a place more remote from sight, with red chalk.

Not long after, Morgiana, whose eyes nothing could escape, went out, and seeing the red chalk, and arguing with herself as she had done before, marked the other neighbors' houses in the same place and manner.

The robber, on his return to his company, valued himself much on the precaution he had taken, which he looked upon as an infallible way of distinguishing Ali Baba's house from the others; and the captain and all of them thought it must succeed. They conveyed themselves into the town with the same precaution as before; but when the robber and his captain came to the street, they found the same difficulty; at which the captain was enraged, and the robber in as great confusion as his predecessor.

Thus the captain and his troop were forced to retire a second time, and much more dissatisfied; while the robber who had been the author of the mistake underwent the same punishment, which he willingly submitted to.

The captain, having lost two brave fellows of his troop, was afraid of diminishing it too much by pursuing this plan to get information of the residence of their plunderer. He found by their example that their heads were not so good as their hands on such occasions; and therefore resolved to take upon himself the important commission.

Accordingly, he went and addressed himself to Baba Mustapha, who did him the same service he had done to the other robbers. He did not set any particular mark on the house, but examined and observed it so carefully, by passing often by it, that it was impossible for him to mistake it.

The captain, well satisfied with his attempt, and informed of what he wanted to know, returned to the forest: and when he came into the cave, where the troop waited for him, said, "Now, comrades, nothing can prevent our full revenge, as I am certain of the house; and on my way hither I have thought how to put it into execution, but if anyone can form a better expedient, let him communicate it."

He then told them his contrivance; and as they approved of it, ordered them to go into the villages about, and buy nineteen mules, with thirty-eight large leather jars, one full of oil, and the others empty.

In two or three days' time the robbers had purchased the mules and jars, and as the mouths of the jars were rather too narrow for his purpose, the captain caused them to be widened, and after having put one of his men into each, with the weapons which he thought fit, leaving open the seam which had been undone to leave them room to breathe, he rubbed the jars on the outside with oil from the full vessel.

Things being thus prepared, when the nineteen mules were loaded with thirty-seven robbers in jars, and the jar of oil, the captain, as their driver, set out with them, and reached the town by the dusk of the evening, as he had intended. He led them through the streets, till he came to Ali Baba's, at whose door he designed to have knocked; but was prevented by his sitting there after supper to take a little fresh air. He stopped his mules, addressed himself to him, and said, "I have brought some oil a great way, to sell at tomorrow's market; and it is now so late that I do not know where to lodge. If I should not be troublesome to you, do me the favor to let me pass the night with you, and I shall be very much obliged by your hospitality."

Though Ali Baba had seen the captain of the robbers in the forest, and had heard him speak, it was impossible to know him in the disguise of an oil merchant. He told him he should be welcome, and immediately opened his gates for the mules to go into the yard. At the same time he called to a slave, and ordered him, when the mules were unloaded, to put them into the stable, and to feed them; and then went to Morgiana, to bid her get a good supper for his guest.

After they had finished supper, Ali Baba, charging Morgiana afresh to take care of his guest, said to her, "To-morrow morning I design to go to the bath before day; take care my bathing linen be ready, give them to Abdalla (which was the slave's name), and make me some good broth against I return." After this he went to bed.

In the meantime the captain of the robbers went into the yard, and took off the lid of each jar, and gave his people orders what to do. Beginning at the first jar, and so on to the last, he said to each man: "As soon as I throw some stones out of the chamber window where I lie, do not fail to come out, and I will immediately join you."

After this he returned into the house, when Morgiana, taking up a light, conducted him to his chamber, where she left him; and he, to avoid any suspicion, put the light out soon after, and laid himself down in his clothes, that he might be the more ready to rise.

Morgiana, remembering Ali Baba's orders, got his bathing linen ready, and ordered Abdalla to set on the pot for the broth; but while she was preparing it the lamp went out, and there was no more oil in the house, nor any candles. What to do she did not know, for the broth must be made. Abdalla, seeing her very uneasy, said, "do not fret and tease yourself, but go into the yard, and take some oil out of one of the jars."

Morgiana thanked Abdalla for his advice, took the oil pot, and went into the yard; when, as she came nigh the first jar, the robber within said softly, "Is it time?"

Though naturally much surprised at finding a man in the jar instead of the oil she wanted, she immediately felt the importance of keeping silence, as Ali Baba, his family, and herself were in great danger; and collecting herself, without showing the least emotion, she answered, "Not yet, but presently." She went quietly in this manner to all the jars, giving the same answer, till she came to the jar of oil.

By this means Morgiana found that her master Ali Baba had admitted thirty-eight robbers into his house, and that this pretended oil merchant was their captain. She made what haste she could to fill her oil pot, and returned into the kitchen, where, as soon as she had lighted her lamp, she took a great kettle, went again to the oil jar, filled the kettle, set it on a large wood fire, and as soon as it boiled, went and poured enough into every jar to stifle and destroy the robber within.

When this action, worthy of the courage of Morgiana, was executed without any noise, as she had projected, she returned into the kitchen with the empty kettle; and having put out the great fire she had made to boil the oil, and leaving just enough to make the broth, put out the lamp also, and remained silent, resolving not to go to rest till, through a window of the kitchen, which opened into the yard, she had seen what might follow.

She had not waited long before the captain of the robbers got up, opened the window, and, finding no light and hearing no noise or any one stirring in the house, gave the appointed signal, by throwing little stones, several of which hit the jars, as he doubted not by the sound they gave. He then listened, but not hearing or perceiving anything whereby he could judge that his companions stirred, he began to grow very uneasy, threw stones again a second and also a third time, and could not comprehend the reason that none of them should answer his signal. Much alarmed, he went softly down into the yard, and going to the first jar, while asking the robber, whom he thought alive, if he was in readiness, smelt the hot boiled oil, which sent forth a steam out of the jar. Hence he knew that his plot to murder Ali Baba and plunder his house was discovered. Examining all the jars, one after another, he found that all his gang were dead; and, enraged to despair at having failed in his design, he forced the lock of a door that led from the yard to the garden, and climbing over the walls made his escape.

When Morgiana saw him depart, she went to bed, satisfied and pleased to have succeeded so well in saving her master and family.

Ali Baba rose before day, and, followed by his slave, went to the baths, entirely ignorant of the important event which had happened at home.

When he returned from the baths he was very much surprised to see the oil jars, and to learn that the merchant was not gone with the mules. He asked Morgiana, who opened the door, the reason of it.

"My good master," answered she, "God preserve you and all your family. You will be better informed of what you wish to know when you have seen what I have to show you, if you will follow me."

As soon as Morgiana had shut the door, Ali Baba followed her, when she requested him to look into the first jar, and see if there was any oil. Ali Baba did so, and seeing a man, started back in alarm, and cried out.

"Do not be afraid," said Morgiana; "the man you see there can neither do you nor anybody else any harm. He is dead."

"Ah, Morgiana," said Ali Baba, "what is it you show me? Explain yourself."

"I will," replied Morgiana. "Moderate your astonishment, and do not excite the curiosity of your neighbors; for it is of great importance to keep this affair secret. Look into all the other jars."

Ali Baba examined all the other jars, one after another; and when he came to that which had the oil in it, found it prodigiously sunk, and stood for some time motionless, sometimes looking at the jars and sometimes at Morgiana, without saying a word, so great was his surprise.

At last, when he had recovered himself, he said, "And what is become of the merchant?"

"Merchant!" answered she; "he is as much one as I am. I will tell you who he is, and what is become of him; but you had better hear the story in your own chamber; for it is time for your health that you had your broth after your bathing."

Morgiana then told him all she had done, from the first observing the mark upon the house, to the destruction of the robbers, and the flight of their captain.

Ali Baba and the Forty Thieves

On hearing of these brave deeds from the lips of Morgiana, Ali Baba said to her--"God, by your means, has delivered me from the snares of these robbers laid for my destruction. I owe, therefore, my life to you; and, for the first token of my acknowledgment, I give you your liberty from this moment, till I can complete your recompense as I intend."

Ali Baba's garden was very long, and shaded at the farther end by a great number of large trees. Near these he and the slave Abdalla dug a trench, long and wide enough to hold the bodies of the robbers; and as the earth was light, they were not long in doing it. When this was done, Ali Baba hid the jars and weapons; and as he had no occasion for the mules, he sent them at different times to be sold in the market by his slave.

While Ali Baba was taking these measures the captain of the forty robbers returned to the forest with inconceivable mortification. He did not stay long; the loneliness of the gloomy cavern became frightful to him. He determined, however, to avenge the death of his companions, and to accomplish the death of Ali Baba. For this purpose he returned to the town, and took a lodging in a khan, disguising himself as a merchant in silks. Under this assumed character he gradually conveyed a great many sorts of rich stuffs and fine linen to his lodging from the cavern, but with all the necessary precautions to conceal the place whence he brought them. In order to dispose of the merchandise, when he had thus amassed them together, he took a warehouse, which happened to be opposite to Cassim's, which Ali Baba's son had occupied since the death of his uncle.

He took the name of Cogia Houssain, and, as a newcomer, was, according to custom, extremely civil and complaisant to all the merchants his neighbors. Ali Baba's son was, from his vicinity, one of the first to converse with Cogia Houssain, who strove to cultivate his friendship more particularly. Two or three days after he was settled, Ali Baba came to see his son, and the captain of the robbers recognized him at once, and soon learned from his son who he was. After this he increased his assiduities, caressed him in the most engaging manner, made him some small presents, and often asked him to dine and sup with him, when he treated him very handsomely.

Ali Baba's son did not choose to lie under such obligation to Cogia Houssain; but was so much straitened for want of room in his house that he could not entertain him. He therefore acquainted his father, Ali Baba, with his wish to invite him in return.

Ali Baba with great pleasure took the treat upon himself. "Son," said he, "to-morrow being Friday, which is a day that the shops of such great merchants as Cogia Houssain and yourself are shut, get him to accompany you, and as you pass by my door, call in. I will go and order Morgiana to provide a supper."

The next day Ali Baba's son and Cogia Houssain met by appointment, took their walk, and as they returned, Ali Baba's son led Cogia Houssain through the street where his father lived, and when they came to the house, stopped and knocked at the door.

"This, sir," said he, "is my father's house, who, from the account I have given him of your friendship, charged me to procure him the honor of your acquaintance; and I desire you to add this pleasure to those for which I am already indebted to you."

Though it was the sole aim of Cogia Houssain to introduce himself into Ali Baba's house, that he might kill him without hazarding his own life or making any noise, yet he excused himself, and offered to take his leave; but a slave having opened the door, Ali Baba's son took him obligingly by the hand, and, in a manner, forced him in.

Ali Baba received Cogia Houssain with a smiling countenance, and in the most obliging manner he could wish. He thanked him for all the favors he had done his son; adding, withal, the obligation was the greater as he was a young man, not much acquainted with the world, and that he might contribute to his information.

Cogia Houssain returned the compliment by assuring Ali Baba that though his son might not have acquired the experience of older men, he had good sense equal to the experience of many others. After a little more conversation on different subjects, he offered again to take his leave, when Ali Baba, stopping him, said, "Where are you going, sir, in so much haste? I beg you will do me the honor to sup with me, though my entertainment may not be worthy your acceptance. Such as it is, I heartily offer it."

"Sir," replied Cogia Houssain, "I am thoroughly persuaded of your good will; but the truth is, I can eat no victuals that have any salt in them; therefore judge how I should feel at your table."

"If that is the only reason," said Ali Baba, "it ought not to deprive me of the honor of your company; for, in the first place, there is no salt ever put into my bread, and as to the meat we shall have to-night, I promise you there shall be none in that. Therefore you must do me the favor to stay. I will return immediately."

Ali Baba went into the kitchen, and ordered Morgiana to put no salt to the meat that was to be dressed that night; and to make quickly two or three ragouts besides what he had ordered, but be sure to put no salt in them.

Morgiana, who was always ready to obey her master, could not help being surprised at his strange order.

"Who is this strange man," said she, "who eats no salt with his meat? Your supper will be spoiled, if I keep it back so long."

"Do not be angry, Morgiana," replied Ali Baba. "He is an honest man, therefore do as I bid you."

Morgiana obeyed, though with no little reluctance, and had a curiosity to see this man who ate no salt. To this end, when she had finished what she had to do in the kitchen, she helped Abdalla to carry up the dishes; and looking at Cogia Houssain, she knew him at first sight, notwithstanding his disguise, to be the captain of the robbers, and examining him very carefully, perceived that he had a dagger under his garment.

"I am not in the least amazed," said she to herself, "that this wicked man, who is my master's greatest enemy, would eat no salt with him, since he intends to assassinate him; but I will prevent him."

Morgiana, while they were at supper, determined in her own mind to execute one of the boldest acts ever meditated. When Abdalla came for the dessert of fruit, and had put it with the wine and glasses before Ali Baba, Morgiana retired, dressed herself neatly with a suitable headdress like a dancer, girded her waist with a silver-gilt girdle, to which there hung a poniard with a hilt and guard of the same metal, and put a handsome mask on her face. When she had thus disguised herself, she said to Abdalla, "Take your tabor, and let us go and divert our master and his son's friend, as we do sometimes when he is alone."

Abdalla took his tabor, and played all the way into the hall before Morgiana, who, when she came to the door, made a low obeisance by way of asking leave to exhibit her skill, while Abdalla left off playing.

"Come in, Morgiana," said Ali Baba, "and let Cogia Houssain see what you can do, that he may tell us what he thinks of your performance."

Cogia Houssain, who did not expect this diversion after supper, began to fear he should not be able to take advantage of the opportunity he thought he had found; but hoped, if he now missed his aim, to secure it another time, by keeping up a friendly correspondence with the father and son; therefore, though he could have wished Ali Baba would have declined the dance, he pretended to be obliged to him for it, and had the complaisance to express his satisfaction at what he saw, which pleased his host.

As soon as Abdalla saw that Ali Baba and Cogia Houssain had done talking, he began to play on the tabor, and accompanied it with an air, to which Morgiana, who was an excellent performer, danced in such a manner as would have created admiration in any company.

After she had danced several dances with much grace, she drew the poniard, and holding it in her hand, began a dance in which she outdid herself by the many different figures, light movements, and the surprising leaps and wonderful exertions with which she accompanied it. Sometimes she presented the poniard to one breast, sometimes to another, and oftentimes seemed to strike her own. At last, she snatched the tabor from Abdalla with her left hand, and holding the dagger in her right presented the other side of the tabor, after the manner of those who get a livelihood by dancing, and solicit the liberality of the spectators.

Ali Baba put a piece of gold into the tabor, as did also his son; and Cogia Houssain, seeing that she was coming to him, had pulled his purse out of his bosom to make her a present; but while he was putting his hand into it, Morgiana, with a courage and resolution worthy of herself, plunged the poniard into his heart.

Ali Baba and his son, shocked at this action, cried out aloud.

"Unhappy woman!" exclaimed Ali Baba, "what have you done, to ruin me and my family?"

"It was to preserve, not to ruin you," answered Morgiana; "for see here," continued she, opening the pretended Cogia Houssain's garment, and showing the dagger, "what an enemy you had entertained! Look well at him, and you will find him to be both the fictitious oil merchant, and the captain of the gang of forty robbers. Remember, too, that he would eat no salt with you; and what would you have more to persuade you of his wicked design? Before I saw him, I suspected him as soon as you told me you had such a guest. I knew him, and you now find that my suspicion was not groundless."

Ali Baba and the Forty Thieves

Ali Baba, who immediately felt the new obligation he had to Morgiana for saving his life a second time, embraced her: "Morgiana," said he, "I gave you your liberty, and then promised you that my gratitude should not stop there, but that I would soon give you higher proofs of its sincerity, which I now do by making you my daughter-in-law."

Then addressing himself to his son, he said, "I believe you, son, to be so dutiful a child, that you will not refuse Morgiana for your wife. You see that Cogia Houssain sought your friendship with a treacherous design to take away my life; and if he had succeeded, there is no doubt but he would have sacrificed you also to his revenge. Consider, that by marrying Morgiana you marry the preserver of my family and your own."

The son, far from showing any dislike, readily consented to the marriage; not only because he would not disobey his father, but also because it was agreeable to his inclination. After this they thought of burying the captain of the robbers with his comrades, and did it so privately that nobody discovered their bones till many years after, when no one had any concern in the publication of this remarkable history. A few days afterward, Ali Baba celebrated the nuptials of his son and Morgiana with great solemnity, a sumptuous feast, and the usual dancing and spectacles; and had the satisfaction to see that his friends and neighbors, whom he invited, had no knowledge of the true motives of the marriage; but that those who were not unacquainted with Morgiana's good qualities commended his generosity and goodness of heart. Ali Baba did not visit the robber's cave for a whole year, as he supposed the other two, whom he could get no account of, might be alive.

At the year's end, when he found they had not made any attempt to disturb him, he had the curiosity to make another journey. He mounted his horse, and when he came to the cave he alighted, tied his horse to a tree, and approaching the entrance, pronounced the words, "Open, Sesame!" and the door opened. He entered the cavern, and by the condition he found things in, judged that nobody had been there since the captain had fetched the goods for his shop. From this time he believed he was the only person in the world who had the secret of opening the cave, and that all the treasure was at his sole disposal. He put as much gold into his saddle-bag as his horse would carry, and returned to town. Some years later he carried his son to the cave, and taught him the secret, which he handed down to his posterity, who, using their good fortune with moderation, lived in great honor and splendor.

The Story of Sindbad the Sailor

In the reign of the same caliph, Haroun al Raschid, of whom we have already heard, there lived at Bagdad a poor porter, called Hindbad. One day, when the weather was excessively hot, he was employed to carry a heavy burden from one end of the town to the other. Being much fatigued, he took off his load, and sat upon it, near a large mansion.

He was much pleased that he stopped at this place, for the agreeable smell of wood of aloes and of pastils, that came from the house, mixing with the scent of the rose water, completely perfumed and embalmed the air. Besides, he heard from within a concert of instrumental music, accompanied with the harmonious notes of nightingales and other birds. This charming melody, and the smell of several sorts of savory dishes, made the porter conclude there was a feast, with great rejoicings within. His business seldom leading him that way, he knew not to whom the mansion belonged; but he went to some of the servants, whom he saw standing at the gate in magnificent apparel, and asked the name of the proprietor.

"How," replied one of them, "do you live in Bagdad, and know not that this is the house of Sindbad the sailor, that famous voyager, who has sailed round the world?"

The porter lifted up his eyes to heaven, and said, loud enough to be heard, "Almighty Creator of all things, consider the difference between Sindbad and me! I am every day exposed to fatigues and calamities, and can scarcely get coarse barley bread for myself and my family, while happy Sindbad profusely expends immense riches, and leads a life of continual pleasure. What has he done to obtain from Thee a lot so agreeable? And what have I done to deserve one so wretched?"

While the porter was thus indulging his melancholy, a servant came out of the house, and taking him by the arm, bade him follow him, for Sindbad, his master, wanted to speak to him.

The servant brought him into a great hall, where a number of people sat round a table covered with all sorts of savory dishes. At the upper end sat a comely, venerable gentleman, with a long white beard, and behind him stood a number of officers and domestics, all ready to attend his pleasure. This person was Sindbad. Hindbad, whose fear was increased at the sight of so many people, and of a banquet so sumptuous, saluted the company, trembling. Sindbad bade him draw near, and seating him at his right hand, served him himself, and gave him excellent wine, of which there was abundance upon the sideboard.

Now Sindbad had himself heard the porter complain through the window, and this it was that induced him to have him brought in. When the repast was over, Sindbad addressed his conversation to Hindbad, and inquired his name and employment, and said, "I wish to hear from your own mouth what it was you lately said in the street."

At this request, Hindbad hung down his head in confusion, and replied, "My lord, I confess that my fatigue put me out of humor and occasioned me to utter some indiscreet words, which I beg you to pardon."

"Do not think I am so unjust," resumed Sindbad, "as to resent such a complaint. But I must rectify your error concerning myself. You think, no doubt, that I have acquired without labor and trouble the ease and indulgence which I now enjoy. But do not mistake; I did not attain to this happy condition without enduring for several years more trouble of body and mind than can well be imagined. Yes, gentlemen," he added, speaking to the whole company, "I assure you that my sufferings have been of a nature so extraordinary as would deprive the greatest miser of his love of riches; and as an opportunity now offers, I will, with your leave, relate the dangers I have encountered, which I think will not be uninteresting to you."

The First Voyage
Of Sindbad the Sailor

My Father was a wealthy merchant of much repute. He bequeathed me a large estate, which I wasted in riotous living. I quickly perceived my error, and that I was misspending my time, which is of all things the most valuable. I remembered the saying of the great Solomon, which I had frequently heard from my father, "A good name is better than precious ointment," and again, "Wisdom is good with an inheritance." Struck with these reflections, I resolved to walk in my father's ways, and I entered into a contract with some merchants, and embarked with them on board a ship we had jointly fitted out.

We set sail, and steered our course toward the Indies, through the Persian Gulf, which is formed by the coasts of Arabia Felix on the right, and by those of Persia on the left. At first I was troubled with seasickness, but speedily recovered my health, and was not afterward subject to that complaint.

In our voyage we touched at several islands, where we sold or exchanged our goods. One day, while under sail, we were becalmed near a small island, but little elevated above the level of the water, and resembling a green meadow. The captain ordered his sails to be furled, and permitted such persons as were so inclined to land; of this number I was one.

But while we were enjoying ourselves in eating and drinking, and recovering ourselves from the fatigue of the sea, the island on a sudden trembled, and shook us terribly.

The trembling of the island was perceived on board the ship, and we were called upon to re-embark speedily, or we should all be lost; for what we took for an island proved to be the back of a sea monster. The nimblest got into the sloop, others betook themselves to swimming; but as for myself, I was still upon the island when it disappeared into the sea, and I had only time to catch hold of a piece of wood that we had brought out of the ship to make a fire. Meanwhile the captain, having received those on board who were in the sloop, and taken up some of those that swam, resolved to improve the favorable gale that had just risen, and hoisting his sails pursued his voyage, so that it was impossible for me to recover the ship.

Thus was I exposed to the mercy of the waves all the rest of the day and the following night. By this time I found my strength gone, and despaired of saving my life, when happily a wave threw me against an island. The bank was high and rugged, so that I could scarcely have got up had it not been for some roots of trees which I found within reach. When the sun arose, though I was very feeble, both from hard labor and want of food, I crept along to find some herbs fit to eat, and had the good luck not only to procure some, but likewise to discover a spring of excellent water, which contributed much to recover me. After this I advanced farther into the island, and at last reached a fine plain, where I perceived some horses feeding. I went toward them, when I heard the voice of a man, who immediately appeared, and asked me who I was. I related to him my adventure, after which, taking me by the hand, he led me into a cave, where there were several other people, no less amazed to see me than I was to see them.

I partook of some provisions which they offered me. I then asked them what they did in such a desert place; to which they answered that they were grooms belonging to the maharaja, sovereign of the island, and that every year they brought thither the king's horses for pasturage. They added that they were to return home on the morrow, and had I been one day later I must have perished, because the inhabited part of the island was a great distance off, and it would have been impossible for me to have got thither without a guide.

Next morning they returned to the capital of the island, took me with them, and presented me to the maharaja. He asked me who I was, and by what adventure I had come into his dominions. After I had satisfied him, he told me he was much concerned for my misfortune, and at the same time ordered that I should want for nothing; which commands his officers were so generous and careful as to see exactly fulfilled.

Being a merchant, I frequented men of my own profession, and particularly inquired for those who were strangers, that perchance I might hear news from Bagdad, or find an opportunity to return. For the maharaja's capital is situated on the seacoast, and has a fine harbor, where ships arrive daily from the different quarters of the world. I frequented also the society of the learned Indians, and took delight to hear them converse; but withal, I took care to make my court regularly to the maharaja, and conversed with the governors and petty kings, his tributaries, that were about him. They put a thousand questions respecting my country; and I, being willing to inform myself as to their laws and customs, asked them concerning everything which I thought worth knowing.

There belongs to this king an island named Cassel. They assured me that every night a noise of drums was heard there, whence the mariners fancied that it was the residence of Gegial.

Sindbad the Sailor

I determined to visit this wonderful place, and in my way thither saw fishes of one hundred and two hundred cubits long, that occasion more fear than hurt; for they are so timorous that they will fly upon the rattling of two sticks or boards. I saw likewise other fish, about a cubit in length, that had heads like owls.

As I was one day at the port after my return, the ship arrived in which I had embarked at Bussorah. I at once knew the captain, and I went and asked him for my bales. "I am Sindbad," said I, "and those bales marked with his name are mine."

When the captain heard me speak thus, "Heavens!" he exclaimed, "whom can we trust in these times! I saw Sindbad perish with my own eyes, as did also the passengers on board, and yet you tell me you are that Sindbad. What impudence is this! And what a false tale to tell, in order to possess yourself of what does not belong to you!"

"Have patience," replied I. "Do me the favor to hear what I have to say."

The captain was at length persuaded that I was no cheat; for there came people from his ship who knew me, paid me great compliments, and expressed much joy at seeing me alive. At last he recollected me himself, and embracing me, "Heaven be praised," said he, "for your happy escape! I cannot express the

joy it affords me. There are your goods; take and do with them as you please."

I took out what was most valuable in my bales, and presented them to the maharaja, who, knowing my misfortune, asked me how I came by such rarities. I acquainted him with the circumstance of their recovery. He was pleased at my good luck, accepted my present, and in return gave me one much more considerable. Upon this I took leave of him, and went aboard the same ship after I had exchanged my goods for the commodities of that country. I carried with me wood of aloes, sandals, camphor, nutmegs, cloves, pepper, and ginger. We passed by several islands, and at last arrived at Bussorah, from whence I came to this city, with the value of one hundred thousand sequins.

Sindbad stopped here, and ordered the musicians to proceed with their concert, which the story had interrupted. When it was evening, Sindbad sent for a purse of one hundred sequins, and giving it to the porter, said, "Take this, Hindbad, return to your home, and come back to-morrow to hear more of my adventures."

The porter went away, astonished at the honor done him, and the present made him. The account of this adventure proved very agreeable to his wife and children, who did not fail to return thanks for what Providence had sent them by the hand of Sindbad.

Hindbad put on his best robe next day, and returned to the bountiful traveler, who received him with a pleasant air, and welcomed him heartily. When all the guests had arrived, dinner was served, and continued a long time.

When it was ended, Sindbad, addressing himself to the company, said, "Gentlemen, be pleased to listen to the adventures of my second voyage. They deserve your attention even more than those of the first." Upon which every one held his peace, and Sindbad proceeded.

The Second Voyage
Of Sindbad the Sailor

I designed, after my first voyage, to spend the rest of my days at Bagdad, but it was not long ere I grew weary of an indolent life, and I put to sea a second time, with merchants of known probity. We embarked on board a good ship, and, after recommending ourselves to God, set sail. We traded from island to island, and exchanged commodities with great profit. One day we landed on an island covered with several sorts of fruit trees, but we could see neither man nor animal. We walked in the meadows, along the streams that watered them. While some diverted themselves with gathering flowers, and others fruits, I took my wine and provisions, and sat down near a stream betwixt two high trees, which formed a thick shade. I made a good meal, and afterward fell sleep. I cannot tell how long I slept, but when I awoke the ship was gone.

In this sad condition I was ready to die with grief. I cried out in agony, beat my head and breast, and threw myself upon the ground, where I lay some time in despair. I upbraided myself a hundred times for not being content with the produce of my first voyage, that might have sufficed me all my life. But all this was in vain, and my repentance came too late. At last I resigned myself to the will of God. Not knowing what to do, I climbed to the top of a lofty tree, from whence I looked about on all sides, to see if I could discover anything that could give me hope. When I gazed toward the sea I could see nothing but sky and water; but looking over the land, I beheld something white; and coming down, I took what provision I had left and went toward it, the distance being so great that I could not distinguish what it was.

As I approached, I thought it to be a white dome, of a prodigious height and extent; and when I came up to it, I touched it, and found it to be very smooth. I went round to see if it was open on any side, but saw it was not, and that there was no climbing up to the top, as it was so smooth. It was at least fifty paces round.

By this time the sun was about to set, and all of a sudden the sky became as dark as if it had been covered with a thick cloud. I was much astonished at this sudden darkness, but much more when I found it was occasioned by a bird of a monstrous size, that came flying toward me. I remembered that I had often heard mariners speak of a miraculous bird called the roc and conceived that the great dome which I so much admired must be its egg. In short, the bird alighted, and sat over the egg. As I perceived her coming, I crept close to the egg, so that I had before me one of the legs of the bird, which was as big as the trunk of a tree. I tied myself strongly to it with my turban, in hopes that the roc next morning would carry me with her out of this desert island. After having passed the night in this condition, the bird flew away as soon as it was daylight, and carried me so high that I could not discern the earth; she afterward descended with so much rapidity that I lost my senses. But when I found myself on the ground, I speedily untied the knot, and had scarcely done so, when the roc, having taken up a serpent of a monstrous length in her bill, flew away.

The spot where it left me was encompassed on all sides by mountains, that seemed to reach above the clouds, and so steep that there was no possibility of getting out of the valley. This was a new perplexity; so that when I compared this place with the desert island from which the roc had brought me, I found that I had gained nothing by the change.

As I walked through this valley, I perceived it was strewn with diamonds, some of which were of surprising bigness. I took pleasure in looking upon them; but shortly I saw at a distance such objects as greatly diminished my satisfaction, and which I could not view without terror, namely, a great number of serpents, so monstrous that the least of them was capable of swallowing an elephant. They retired in the daytime to their dens, where they hid themselves from the roc, their enemy, and came out only in the night.

I spent the day in walking about in the valley, resting myself at times in such places as I thought most convenient. When night came on I went into a cave, where I thought I might repose in safety. I secured the entrance, which was low and narrow, with a great stone, to preserve me from the serpents; but not so far as to exclude the light. I supped on part of my provisions, but the serpents, which began hissing round me, put me into such extreme fear that I did not sleep. When day appeared the serpents retired, and I came out of the cave, trembling. I can justly say that I walked upon diamonds without feeling any inclination to touch them. At last I sat down, and notwithstanding my apprehensions, not having closed my eyes during the night, fell asleep, after having eaten a little more of my provisions. But I had scarcely shut my eyes when something that fell by me with a great noise awakened me. This was a large piece of raw meat; and at the same time I saw several others fall down from the rocks in different places. I had always regarded as fabulous what I had heard sailors and others relate of the valley of diamonds, and of the stratagems employed by merchants to obtain jewels from thence; but now I found that they had stated nothing but the truth. For the fact is, that the merchants come to the neighborhood of this valley, when the eagles have young ones, and throwing great joints of meat into the valley, the diamonds, upon whose points they fall, stick to them; the eagles, which are stronger in this country than anywhere else, pounce with great force upon those pieces of meat, and carry them to their nests on the precipices of the rocks to feed their young: the merchants at this time run to their nests, disturb and drive off the eagles by their shouts, and take away the diamonds that stick to the meat.

I perceived in this device the means of my deliverance.

Having collected together the largest diamonds I could find, and put them into the leather bag in which I used to carry my provisions, I took the largest of the pieces of meat, tied it close round me with the cloth of my turban, and then laid myself upon the ground, with my face downward, the bag of diamonds being made fast to my girdle.

I had scarcely placed myself in this posture when one of the eagles, having taken me up with the piece of meat to which I was fastened, carried me to his nest on the top of the mountain. The merchants immediately began their shouting to frighten the eagles; and when they had obliged them to quit their prey, one of them came to the nest where I was. He was much alarmed when he saw me; but recovering himself, instead of inquiring how I came thither, began to quarrel with me, and asked why I stole his goods.

"You will treat me," replied I, "with more civility when you know me better. Do not be uneasy; I have diamonds enough for you and myself, more than all the other merchants together. Whatever they have they owe to chance; but I selected for myself, in the bottom of the valley, those which you see in this bag."

I had scarcely done speaking, when the other merchants came crowding about us, much astonished to see me; but they were much more surprised when I told them my story.

They conducted me to their encampment; and there, having opened my bag, they were surprised at the largeness of my diamonds, and confessed that they had never seen any of such size and perfection. I prayed the merchant who owned the nest to which I had been carried (for every merchant had his own) to take as many for his share as he pleased. He contented himself with one, and that, too, the least of them; and when I pressed him to take more, without fear of doing me any injury, "No," said he, "I am very well satisfied with this, which is valuable enough to save me the trouble of making any more voyages, and will raise as great a fortune as I desire."

I spent the night with the merchants, to whom I related my story a second time, for the satisfaction of those who had not heard it. I could not moderate my joy when I found myself delivered from the danger I have mentioned. I thought myself in a dream, and could scarcely believe myself out of danger.

The merchants had thrown their pieces of meat into the valley for several days; and each of them being satisfied with the diamonds that had fallen to his lot, we left the place the next morning, and traveled near high mountains, where there were serpents of a prodigious length, which we had the good fortune to escape. We took shipping at the first port we reached, and touched at the isle of Roha, where the trees grow that yield camphor. This tree is so large, and its branches so thick, that one hundred men may easily sit under its shade. The juice, of which the camphor is made, exudes from a hole bored in the upper part of the tree, and is received in a vessel, where it thickens to a consistency, and becomes what we call camphor. After the juice is thus drawn out, the tree withers and dies.

In this island is also found the rhinoceros, an animal less than the elephant but larger than the buffalo. It has a horn upon its nose, about a cubit in length; this horn is solid, and cleft through the middle. The rhinoceros fights with the elephant, runs his horn into his belly and carries him off upon his head; but the blood and the fat of the elephant running into his eyes and making him blind, he falls to the ground; and then, strange to relate, the roc comes and carries them both away in her claws, for food for her young ones.

I pass over many other things peculiar to this island, lest I should weary you. Here I exchanged some of my diamonds for merchandise. From hence we went to other islands, and at last, having touched at several trading towns of the continent, we landed at Bussorah, from whence I proceeded to Bagdad. There I immediately gave large presents to the poor, and lived honorably upon the vast riches I had brought, and gained with so much fatigue.

Thus Sindbad ended the relation of the second voyage, gave Hindbad another hundred sequins, and invited him to come the next day to hear the account of the third.

The Third Voyage
Of Sindbad the Sailor

I soon again grew weary of living a life of idleness, and hardening myself against the thought of any danger, I embarked with some merchants on another long voyage. We touched at several ports, where we traded. One day we were overtaken by a dreadful tempest, which drove us from our course. The storm continued several days, and brought us before the port of an island, which the captain was very unwilling to enter; but we were obliged to cast anchor. When we had furled our sails the captain told us that this and some other neighboring islands were inhabited by hairy savages, who would speedily attack us; and though they were but dwarfs we must make no resistance, for they were more in number than the locusts; and if we happened to kill one, they would all fall upon us and destroy us.

We soon found that what the captain had told us was but too true. An innumerable multitude of frightful savages, about two feet high, covered all over with red hair, came swimming toward us, and encompassed our ship. They chattered as they came near, but we understood not their language. They climbed up the sides of the ship with such agility as surprised us. They took down our sails, cut the cable, and hauling to the shore, made us all get out, and afterward carried the ship into another island, from whence they had come.

As we advanced, we perceived at a distance a vast pile of building, and made toward it. We found it to be a palace, elegantly built, and very lofty, with a gate of ebony of two leaves, which we opened. We saw before us a large apartment, with a porch, having on one side a heap of human bones, and on

105

the other a vast number of roasting spits. We trembled at this spectacle, and were seized with deadly apprehension, when suddenly the gate of the apartment opened with a loud crash, and there came out the horrible figure of a black man, as tall as a lofty palm tree. He had but one eye, and that in the middle of his forehead, where it blazed bright as a burning coal. His foreteeth were very long and sharp, and stood out of his mouth, which was as deep as that of a horse. His upper lip hung down upon his breast. His ears resembled those of an elephant, and covered his shoulders; and his nails were as long and crooked as the talons of the greatest birds. At the sight of so frightful a genie we became insensible, and lay like dead men.

At last we came to ourselves, and saw him sitting in the porch looking at us. When he had considered us well, he advanced toward us, and laying his hand upon me, took me up by the nape of my neck, and turned me around, as a butcher would do a sheep's head. After having examined me, and perceiving me to be so lean that I was nothing but skin and bone, he let me go. He took up all the rest one by one, and viewed them in the same manner. The captain being the fattest, he held him with one hand, as I would do a sparrow, and thrust a spit through him; he then kindled a great fire, roasted, and ate him in his apartment for his supper. Having finished his repast, he returned to his porch, where he lay and fell asleep, snoring louder than thunder. He slept thus till morning. As for ourselves, it was not possible for us to enjoy any rest, so that we passed the night in the most painful apprehension that can be imagined. When day appeared the giant awoke, got up, went out, and left us in the palace.

The next night we determined to revenge ourselves on the brutish giant, and did so in the following manner. After he had again finished his inhuman supper on another of our seamen, he

lay down on his back, and fell asleep. As soon as we heard him
snore according to his custom, nine of the boldest among us, and
myself, took each of us a spit, and putting the points of them into
the fire till they were burning hot, we thrust them into his eye all
at once, and blinded him. The pain made him break out into a
frightful yell: he started up, and stretched out his hands in order
to sacrifice some of us to his rage, but we ran to such places as
he could not reach; and after having sought for us in vain, he
groped for the gate, and went out, howling in agony.

We immediately left the palace, and came to the shore, where
with some timber that lay about in great quantities, we made
some rafts, each large enough to carry three men. We waited
until day to get upon them, for we hoped if the giant did not
appear by sunrise, and give over his howling, which we still
heard, that he would prove to be dead; and if that happened to be
the case, we resolved to stay on that island, and not to risk our
lives upon the rafts. But day had scarcely appeared when we
perceived our cruel enemy, with two others, almost of the same
size, leading him; and a great number more coming before him
at a quick pace.

We did not hesitate to take to our rafts, but put to sea with all the
speed we could. The giants, who perceived this, took up great
stones, and running to the shore they entered the water up to the
middle, and threw so exactly that they sank all the rafts but that I
was upon; and all my companions, except the two with me, were
drowned. We rowed with all our might, and got out of the reach
of the giants. But when we got out to sea we were exposed to the
mercy of the waves and winds, and spent that day and the
following night under the most painful uncertainty as to our fate;
but next morning we had the good fortune to be thrown upon an

island, where we landed with much joy. We found excellent fruit, which afforded us great relief, and recruited our strength.

At night we went to sleep on the seashore; but were awakened by the noise of a serpent of surprising length and thickness, whose scales made a rustling noise as he wound himself along. It swallowed up one of my comrades, notwithstanding his loud cries and the efforts he made to extricate himself from it. Dashing him several times against the ground, it crushed him, and we could hear it gnaw and tear the poor fellow's bones, though we had fled to a considerable distance. The following day, to our great terror, we saw the serpent again, when I exclaimed, "O Heaven, to what dangers are we exposed! We rejoiced yesterday at having escaped from the cruelty of a giant and the rage of the waves; now are we fallen into another danger equally dreadful."

As we walked about, we saw a large tall tree, upon which we designed to pass the following night for our security; and having satisfied our hunger with fruit, we mounted it accordingly. Shortly after, the serpent came hissing to the foot of the tree, raised itself up against the trunk of it, and meeting with my comrade, who sat lower than I, swallowed him at once, and went off.

I remained upon the tree till it was day, and then came down, more like a dead man than one alive, expecting the same fate as had befallen my two companions. This filled me with horror, and I advanced some steps to throw myself into the sea; but I withstood this dictate of despair, and submitted myself to the will of God, who disposes of our lives at His pleasure.

In the meantime I collected together a great quantity of small wood, brambles, and dry thorns, and making them up into bundles, made a wide circle with them round the tree, and also tied some of them to the branches over my head. Having done this, when the evening came I shut myself up within this circle, with the melancholy satisfaction that I had neglected nothing which could preserve me from the cruel destiny with which I was threatened. The serpent failed not to come at the usual hour, and went round the tree, seeking for an opportunity to devour me, but was prevented by the rampart I had made; so that he lay till day, like a cat watching in vain for a mouse that has fortunately reached a place of safety. When day appeared, he retired, but I dared not leave my fort until the sun arose.

God took compassion on my hopeless state; for just as I was going, in a fit of desperation, to throw myself into the sea, I perceived a ship in the distance. I called as loud as I could, and unfolding the linen of my turban, displayed it, that they might observe me. This had the desired effect. The crew perceived me, and the captain sent his boat for me.

As soon as I came on board, the merchants and seamen flocked about me, to know how I came into that desert island; and after I had related to them all that had befallen me, the oldest among them said they had several times heard of the giants that dwelt on that island, and that they were cannibals; and as to the serpents, they added that there were abundant in the island; that they hid themselves by day, and came abroad by night. After having testified their joy at my escaping so many dangers, they brought me the best of their provisions; and took me before the captain, who, seeing that I was in rags, gave me one of his own suits. Looking steadfastly upon him, I knew him to be the person who, on my second voyage, had left me in the island where I fell asleep, and had sailed without me, or without sending to seek for me.

I was not surprised that he, believing me to be dead, did not recognize me.

"Captain," said I, "look at me, and you may know that I am Sindbad, whom you left in that desert island."

The captain, having considered me attentively, recognized me.

"God be praised!" said he, embracing me; "I rejoice that fortune has rectified my fault. There are your goods, which I always took care to preserve."

I took them from him, and made him my acknowledgments for his care of them.

We continued at sea for some time, touched at several islands, and at last landed at that of Salabat, where sandalwood is obtained, which is much used in medicine.

From the isle of Salabat we went to another, where I furnished myself with cloves, cinnamon, and other spices. As we sailed from this island we saw a tortoise twenty cubits in length and breadth. We observed also an amphibious animal like a cow, which gave milk; its skin is so hard, that they usually make bucklers of it. I saw another, which had the shape and color of a camel

In short, after a long voyage I arrived at Bussorah, and from thence returned to Bagdad with so much wealth that I knew not its extent. I gave a great deal to the poor, and bought another considerable estate.

Thus Sindbad finished the history of his third voyage. He gave another hundred sequins to Hindbad, and invited him to dinner again the next day, to hear

The Fourth Voyage
Of Sindbad the Sailor

After I had rested from the dangers of my third voyage, my passion for trade and my love of novelty soon again prevailed. I therefore settled my affairs, and provided a stock of goods fit for the traffic I designed to engage in. I took the route to Persia, traveled over several provinces, and then arrived at a port, where I embarked. On putting out to sea, we were overtaken by such a sudden gust of wind as obliged the captain to lower his yards, and take all other necessary precautions to prevent the danger that threatened us. But all was in vain; our endeavors had no effect. The sails were split in a thousand pieces, and the ship was stranded, several of the merchants and seamen were drowned, and the cargo was lost.

I had the good fortune, with several of the merchants and mariners, to get upon some planks, and we were carried by the current to an island which lay before us. There we found fruit and spring water, which preserved our lives. We stayed all night near the place where we had been cast ashore.

Next morning, as soon as the sun was up, we explored the island, and saw some houses, which we approached. As soon as we drew near we were encompassed by a great number of negroes, who seized us, shared us among them, and carried us to their respective habitations.

I and five of my comrades were carried to one place; here they made us sit down, and gave us a certain herb, which they made signs to us to eat. My comrades, not taking notice that the blacks ate none of it themselves, thought only of satisfying their hunger, and ate with greediness. But I, suspecting some trick, would not so much as taste it, which happened well for me; for in a little time after I perceived my companions had lost their senses, and that when they spoke to me they knew not what they said.

The negroes fed us afterward with rice, prepared with oil of coconuts; and my comrades, who had lost their reason, ate of it greedily. I also partook of it, but very sparingly. They gave us that herb at first on purpose to deprive us of our senses, that we might not be aware of the sad destiny prepared for us; and they supplied us with rice to fatten us; for, being cannibals, their design was to eat us as soon as we grew fat. This accordingly happened, for they devoured my comrades, who were not sensible of their condition; but my senses being entire, you may easily guess that instead of growing fat, as the rest did, I grew leaner every day. The fear of death turned all my food into poison. I fell into a languishing distemper, which proved my safety; for the negroes, having killed and eaten my companions, seeing me to be withered, lean, and sick, deferred my death.

Meanwhile I had much liberty, so that scarcely any notice was taken of what I did, and this gave me an opportunity one day to get at a distance from the houses, and to make my escape. An old man who saw me, and suspected my design, called to me as loud as he could to return; but instead of obeying him, I redoubled my speed, and quickly got out of sight. At that time there was none but the old man about the houses, the rest being abroad, and not to return till night, which was usual with them. Therefore, being sure that they could not arrive in time to pursue me, I went on till night, when I stopped to rest a little, and to eat some of the provisions I had secured; but I speedily set forward again, and traveled seven days, avoiding those places which seemed to be inhabited, and lived for the most part upon coconuts, which served me both for meat and drink. On the eighth day I came near the sea, and saw some white people, like myself, gathering pepper, of which there was great plenty in that place. This I took to be a good omen, and went to them without any scruple.

The people who gathered pepper came to meet me as soon as they saw me, and asked me in Arabic who I was and whence I came. I was overjoyed to hear them speak in my own language, and I satisfied their curiosity by giving them an account of my shipwreck, and how I fell into the hands of the negroes.

"Those negroes," replied they, "eat men; and by what miracle did you escape their cruelty?" I related to them the circumstances I have just mentioned, at which they were wonderfully surprised.

I stayed with them till they had gathered their quantity of pepper, and then sailed with them to the island from whence they had come. They presented me to their king, who was a good prince. He had the patience to hear the relation of my adventures, which surprised him; and he afterward gave me clothes, and commanded care to be taken of me.

The island was very well peopled, plentiful in everything, and the capital a place of great trade. This agreeable retreat was very comfortable to me after my misfortunes, and the kindness of this generous prince completed my satisfaction. In a word, there was not a person more in favor with him than myself, and consequently every man in court and city sought to oblige me; so that in a very little time I was looked upon rather as a native than a stranger.

I observed one thing, which to me appeared very extraordinary. All the people, the king himself not excepted, rode their horses without bridle or stirrups. I went one day to a workman, and gave him a model for making the stock of a saddle. When that was done, I covered it myself with velvet and leather, and embroidered it with gold. I afterward went to a smith, who made me a bit, according to the pattern I showed him, and also some stirrups. When I had all things completed, I presented them to the king, and put them upon one of his horses. His majesty mounted immediately, and was so pleased with them that he testified his satisfaction by large presents. I made several others for the ministers and principal officers of his household, which gained me great reputation and regard.

As I paid my court very constantly to the king, he said to me one day, "Sindbad, I love thee. I have one thing to demand of thee, which thou must grant. I have a mind thou shouldst marry, that so thou mayst stay in my dominions, and think no more of thy own country."

I durst not resist the prince's will, and he gave me one of the ladies of his court, noble, beautiful, and rich. The ceremonies of marriage being over, I went and dwelt with my wife, and for some time we lived together in perfect harmony. I was not, however, satisfied with my banishment. Therefore I designed to make my escape at the first opportunity, and to return to Bagdad, which my present settlement, how advantageous so-ever, could not make me forget.

At this time the wife of one of my neighbors, with whom I had contracted a very strict friendship, fell sick and died. I went to see and comfort him in his affliction, and finding him absorbed in sorrow, I said to him, as soon as I saw him, "God preserve you, and grant you a long life."

"Alas!" replied he, "how do you think I should obtain the favor you wish me? I have not above an hour to live, for I must be buried this day with my wife. This is a law on this island. The living husband is interred with the dead wife, and the living wife with the dead husband."

While he was giving me an account of this barbarous custom, the very relation of which chilled my blood, his kindred, friends, and neighbors came to assist at the funeral. They dressed the corpse of the woman in her richest apparel and all her jewels, as if it had been her wedding day; then they placed her on an open bier, and began their march to the place of burial. The husband walked first, next to the dead body. They proceeded to a high mountain, and when they had reached the place of their destination they took up a large stone which formed the mouth of a deep pit, and let down the body with all its apparel and jewels. Then the husband, embracing his kindred and friends, without resistance suffered himself to be placed on another bier, with a pot of water and seven small loaves, and was let down in the same manner. The ceremony being over, the mouth of the pit was again covered with the stone, and the company returned.

I mention this ceremony the more particularly because I was in a few weeks' time to be the principal actor on a similar occasion. Alas! my own wife fell sick and died. I made every remonstrance I could to the king not to expose me, a foreigner, to this inhuman law. I appealed in vain. The king and all his court, with the most considerable persons of the city, sought to soften my sorrow by honoring the funeral ceremony with their presence; and at the termination of the ceremony I was lowered into the pit with a vessel full of water, and seven loaves. As I approached the bottom I discovered, by the aid of the little light that came from above, the nature of this subterranean place; it seemed an endless cavern, and might be about fifty fathoms deep.

I lived for some time upon my bread and water, when, one day, just as I was on the point of exhaustion, I heard something tread, and breathing or panting as it moved. I followed the sound. The animal seemed to stop sometimes, but always fled and breathed hard as I approached. I pursued it for a considerable time, till at last I perceived a light, resembling a star; I went on, sometimes lost sight of it, but always found it again, and at last discovered that it came through a hole in the rock, which I got through, and found myself upon the seashore, at which I felt exceeding joy. I prostrated myself on the shore to thank God for this mercy, and shortly afterward I perceived a ship making for the place where I was. I made a sign with the linen of my turban, and called to the crew as loud as I could. They heard me, and sent a boat to bring me on board. It was fortunate for me that these people did not inspect the place where they found me, but without hesitation took me on board.

We passed by several islands, and among others that called the Isle of Bells, about ten days' sail from Serendib with a regular wind, and six from that of Kela, where we landed. Lead mines are found in the island; also Indian canes, and excellent camphor.

The King of the Isle of Kela is very rich and powerful, and the Isle of Bells, which is about two days' journey away, is also subject to him. The inhabitants are so barbarous that they still eat human flesh. After we had finished our traffic in that island we put to sea again, and touched at several other ports; at last I arrived happily at Bagdad. Out of gratitude to God for His mercies, I contributed liberally toward the support of several mosques and the subsistence of the poor, and enjoyed myself with my friends in festivities and amusements.

Here Sindbad made a new present of one hundred sequins to Hindbad, whom he requested to return with the rest next day at the same hour, to dine with him and hear the story of his fifth voyage.

The Fifth Voyage
Of Sindbad the Sailor

All the troubles and calamities I had undergone could not cure me of my inclination to make new voyages. I therefore bought goods, departed with them for the best seaport, and there, that I might not be obliged to depend upon a captain, but have a ship at my own command, I remained till one was built on purpose, at my own charge. When the ship was ready I went on board with my goods; but not having enough to load her, I agreed to take with me several merchants of different nations, with their merchandise.

We sailed with the first fair wind, and after a long navigation the first place we touched at was a desert island, where we found the egg of a roc, equal in size to that I formerly mentioned. There was a young roc in it, just ready to be hatched, and its beak had begun to break the egg.

The merchants who landed with me broke the egg with hatchets, and making a hole in it, pulled out the young roc piecemeal, and roasted it. I had in vain entreated them not to meddle with the egg.

Scarcely had they finished their repast, when there appeared in the air, at a considerable distance, two great clouds. The captain of my ship, knowing by experience what they meant, said they were the male and female parents of the roc, and pressed us to re-embark with all speed, to prevent the misfortune which he saw would otherwise befall us.

The two rocs approached with a frightful noise, which they redoubled when they saw the egg broken, and their young one gone. They flew back in the direction they had come, and disappeared for some time, while we made all the sail we could in the endeavor to prevent that which unhappily befell us.

They soon returned, and we observed that each of them carried between its talons an enormous rock. When they came directly over my ship, they hovered, and one of them let go his rock; but by the dexterity of the steersman it missed us and fell into the sea. The other so exactly hit the middle of the ship as to split it into pieces. The mariners and passengers were all crushed to death or fell into the sea. I myself was of the number of the latter; but, as I came up again, I fortunately caught hold of a piece of the wreck, and swimming, sometimes with one hand and sometimes with the other, but always holding fast the plank, the wind and the tide favoring me, I came to an island, and got safely ashore.

I sat down upon the grass, to recover myself from my fatigue, after which I went into the island to explore it. It seemed to be a delicious garden. I found trees everywhere, some of them bearing green and others ripe fruits, and streams of fresh pure water. I ate of the fruits, which I found excellent; and drank of the water, which was very light and good.

When I was a little advanced into the island, I saw an old man, who appeared very weak and infirm. He was sitting on the bank of a stream, and at first I took him to be one who had been shipwrecked like myself. I went toward him and saluted him, but he only slightly bowed his head. I asked him why he sat so still; but instead of answering me, he made a sign for me to take him upon my back, and carry him over the brook.

I believed him really to stand in need of my assistance, took him upon my back, and having carried him over, bade him get down, and for that end stooped, that he might get off with ease; but instead of doing so (which I laugh at every time I think of it), the old man, who to me appeared quite decrepit, threw his legs nimbly about my neck. He sat astride upon my shoulders, and held my throat so tight that I thought he would have strangled me, and I fainted away.

Notwithstanding my fainting, the ill-natured old fellow still kept his seat upon my neck. When I had recovered my breath, he thrust one of his feet against my side, and struck me so rudely with the other that he forced me to rise up, against my will. Having arisen, he made me carry him under the trees, and forced me now and then to stop, that he might gather and eat fruit. He never left his seat all day; and when I lay down to rest at night he laid himself down with me, still holding fast about my neck. Every morning he pinched me to make me awake, and afterward obliged me to get up and walk, and spurred me with his feet.

One day I found several dry calabashes that had fallen from a tree. I took a large one, and after cleaning it, pressed into it some juice of grapes, which abounded in the island. Having filled the calabash, I put it by in a convenient place, and going thither again some days after, I tasted it, and found the wine so good that it gave me new vigor, and so exhilarated my spirits that I began to sing and dance as I carried my burden.

The old man, perceiving the effect which this had upon me, and that I carried him with more ease than before, made me a sign to give him some of it. I handed him the calabash, and the liquor pleasing his palate, he drank it off. There being a considerable quantity of it, he soon began to sing, and to move about from side to side in his seat upon my shoulders, and by degrees to loosen his legs from about me. Finding that he did not press me as before, I threw him upon the ground, where he lay without motion. I then took up a great stone and slew him.

I was extremely glad to be thus freed forever from this troublesome fellow. I now walked toward the beach, where I met the crew of a ship that had cast anchor, to take in water. They were surprised to see me, but more so at hearing the particulars of my adventures.

"You fell," said they, "into the hands of the old man of the sea, and are the first who ever escaped strangling by his malicious embraces. He never quitted those he had once made himself master of, till he had destroyed them, and he has made this island notorious by the number of men he has slain."

They carried me with them to the captain, who received me with great kindness. He put out again to sea, and after some days' sail we arrived at the harbor of a great city, the houses of which overhung the sea.

One of the merchants, who had taken me into his friendship, invited me to go along with him. He gave me a large sack, and having recommended me to some people of the town, who used to gather coconuts, desired them to take me with them.

"Go," said he, "follow them, and act as you see them do; but do not separate from them, otherwise you may endanger your life."

Having thus spoken, he gave me provisions for the journey, and I went with them.

We came to a thick forest of coco palms, very lofty, with trunks so smooth that it was not possible to climb to the branches that bore the fruit. When we entered the forest we saw a great number of apes of several sizes, who fled as soon as they perceived us, and climbed to the tops of the trees with amazing swiftness.

The merchants with whom I was gathered stones, and threw them at the apes on the trees. I did the same; and the apes, out of revenge, threw coconuts at us so fast, and with such gestures, as sufficiently testified their anger and resentment. We gathered up the coconuts, and from time to time threw stones to provoke the apes; so that by this stratagem we filled our bags with coconuts. I thus gradually collected as many coconuts as produced me a considerable sum.

Having laden our vessel with coconuts, we set sail, and passed by the islands where pepper grows in great plenty. From thence we went to the Isle of Comari, where the best species of wood of aloes grows. I exchanged my coconuts in those two islands for pepper and wood of aloes, and went with other merchants pearl fishing. I hired divers, who brought me up some that were very large and pure. I embarked in a vessel that happily arrived at Bussorah; from thence I returned to Bagdad, where I realized vast sums from my pepper, wood of aloes, and pearls. I gave the tenth of my gains in alms, as I had done upon my return from my other voyages, and rested from my fatigues.

Sindbad here ordered one hundred sequins to be given to Hindbad, and requested him and the other guests to dine with him the next day, to hear the account of his sixth voyage.

The Sixth Voyage
Of Sindbad the Sailor

I know, my friends, that you will wish to hear how, after having been shipwrecked five times, and escaped so many dangers, I could resolve again to tempt fortune, and expose myself to new hardships. I am myself astonished at my conduct when I reflect upon it, and must certainly have been actuated by my destiny, from which none can escape. Be that as it may, after a year's rest I prepared for a sixth voyage, notwithstanding the entreaties of my kindred and friends, who did all in their power to dissuade me.

Instead of taking my way by the Persian Gulf I traveled once more through several provinces of Persia and the Indies, and arrived at a seaport. Here I embarked in a ship, the captain of which was bound on a long voyage, in which he and the pilot lost their course. Suddenly we saw the captain quit his rudder, uttering loud lamentations. He threw off his turban, pulled his beard, and beat his head like a madman. We asked him the reason; and he answered that we were in the most dangerous place in all the ocean.

"A rapid current carries the ship along with it, and we shall all perish in less than a quarter of an hour. Pray to God to deliver us from this peril. We cannot escape, if He do not take pity on us."

At these words he ordered the sails to be lowered; but all the ropes broke, and the ship was carried by the current to the foot of an inaccessible mountain, where she struck and went to pieces; yet in such a manner that we saved our lives, our provisions, and the best of our goods.

The mountain at the foot of which we were was covered with wrecks, with a vast number of human bones, and with an incredible quantity of goods and riches of all kinds, These objects served only to augment our despair. In all other places it is usual for rivers to run from their channels into the sea; but here a river of fresh water runs from the sea into a dark cavern, whose entrance is very high and spacious. What is most remarkable in this place is that the stones of the mountain are of crystal, rubies, or other precious stones. Here is also a sort of fountain of pitch or bitumen, that runs into the sea, which the fish swallow, and evacuate soon afterward, turned into ambergris; and this the waves throw up on the beach in great quantities. Trees also grow here, most of which are of wood of aloes, equal in goodness to those of Comari.

To finish the description of this place, it is not possible for ships to get off when once they approach within a certain distance. If they be driven thither by a wind from the sea, the wind and the current impel them; and if they come into it when a land wind blows, which might seem to favor their getting out again, the height of the mountain stops the wind, and occasions a calm, so that the force of the current carries them ashore; and what completes the misfortune is, that there is no possibility of ascending the mountain, or of escaping by sea.

We continued upon the shore, at the foot of the mountain, in a state of despair, and expected death every day. On our first landing we had divided our provisions as equally as we could, and thus every one lived a longer or a shorter time, according to his temperance, and the use he made of his provisions.

I survived all my companions; and when I buried the last I had so little provisions remaining that I thought I could not long survive, and I dug a grave, resolving to lie down in it because there was no one left to pay me the last offices of respect. But it pleased God once more to take compassion on me, and put it in my mind to go to the bank of the river which ran into the great cavern. Considering its probable course with great attention, I said to myself, "This river, which runs thus underground, must somewhere have an issue. If I make a raft, and leave myself to the current, it will convey me to some inhabited country, or I shall perish. If I be drowned, I lose nothing, but only change one kind of death for another."

I immediately went to work upon large pieces of timber and cables, for I had a choice of them from the wrecks, and tied them together so strongly that I soon made a very solid raft. When I had finished, I loaded it with some chests of rubies, emeralds, ambergris, rock-crystal, and bales of rich stuffs. Having balanced my cargo exactly, and fastened it well to the raft, I went on board with two oars that I had made, and leaving it to the course of the river, resigned myself to the will of God.

As soon as I entered the cavern I lost all light, and the stream carried me I knew not whither. Thus I floated on in perfect darkness, and once found the arch so low, that it very nearly touched my head, which made me cautious afterward to avoid the like danger. All this while I ate nothing but what was just necessary to support nature; yet, notwithstanding my frugality, all my provisions were spent. Then I became insensible. I cannot tell how long I continued so; but when I revived, I was surprised to find myself on an extensive plain on the brink of a river, where my raft was tied, amidst a great number of negroes.

I got up as soon as I saw them, and saluted them. They spoke to me, but I did not understand their language. I was so transported with joy that I knew not whether I was asleep or awake; but being persuaded that I was not asleep, I recited the following words in Arabic aloud: "Call upon the Almighty, He will help thee; thou needest not perplex thyself about anything else: shut thy eyes, and while thou art asleep, God will change thy bad fortune into good."

One of the negroes, who understood Arabic, hearing me speak thus, came toward me, and said, "Brother, be not surprised to see us; we are inhabitants of this country, and water our fields from this river, which comes out of the neighboring mountain. We saw your raft, and one of us swam into the river, and brought it hither, where we fastened it, as you see, until you should awake. Pray tell us your history. Whence did you come?"

I begged of them first to give me something to eat, and then I would satisfy their curiosity. They gave me several sorts of food, and when I had satisfied my hunger I related all that had befallen me, which they listened to with attentive surprise. As soon as I had finished, they told me, by the person who spoke Arabic and interpreted to them what I said, that I must go along with them, and tell my story to their king myself, it being too extraordinary to be related by any other than the person to whom the events had happened.

They immediately sent for a horse, and having helped me to mount, some of them walked before to show the way, while the rest took my raft and cargo and followed.

We marched till we came to the capital of Serendib, for it was on that island I had landed. The negroes presented me to their king;

I approached his throne, and saluted him as I used to do the kings of the Indies; that is to say, I prostrated myself at his feet. The prince ordered me to rise, received me with an obliging air, and made me sit down near him.

I concealed nothing from the king, but related to him all that I have told you. At last my raft was brought in, and the bales opened in his presence: he admired the quantity of wood of aloes and ambergris; but, above all, the rubies and emeralds, for he had none in his treasury that equaled them.

Observing that he looked on my jewels with pleasure, and viewed the most remarkable among them, one after another, I fell prostrate at his feet, and took the liberty to say to him, "Sire, not only my person is at your majesty's service, but the cargo of the raft, and I would beg of you to dispose of it as your own."

He answered me with a smile, "Sindbad, I will take nothing of yours; far from lessening your wealth, I design to augment it, and will not let you quit my dominions without marks of my liberality."

He then charged one of his officers to take care of me, and ordered people to serve me at his own expense. The officer was very faithful in the execution of his commission, and caused all the goods to be carried to the lodgings provided for me.

I went every day at a set hour to make my court to the king, and spent the rest of my time in viewing the city, and what was most worthy of notice.

The capital of Serendib stands at the end of a fine valley, in the middle of the island, encompassed by high mountains. They are seen three days' sail off at sea. Rubies and several sorts of minerals abound. All kinds of rare plants and trees grow there, especially cedars and coconut. There is also a pearl fishery in the mouth of its principal river, and in some of its valleys are found diamonds. I made, by way of devotion, a pilgrimage to the place where Adam was confined after his banishment from Paradise, and had the curiosity to go to the top of the mountain.

When I returned to the city I prayed the king to allow me to return to my own country, and he granted me permission in the most obliging and honorable manner. He would force a rich present upon me; and at the same time he charged me with a letter for the Commander of the Faithful, our sovereign, saying to me, "I pray you give this present from me, and this letter, to the Caliph Haroun al Raschid, and assure him of my friendship."

The letter from the King of Serendib was written on the skin of a certain animal of great value, very scarce, and of a yellowish color. The characters of this letter were of azure, and the contents as follows:

"The King of the Indies, before whom march one hundred elephants, who lives in a palace that shines with one hundred thousand rubies, and who has in his treasury twenty thousand crowns enriched with diamonds, to Caliph Haroun al Raschid.

"Though the present we send you be inconsiderable, receive it, however, as a brother and a friend, in consideration of the hearty friendship which we bear for you, and of which we are willing to give you proof. We desire the same part in your friendship, considering that we believe it to be our merit, as we are both kings. We send you this letter as from one brother to another. Farewell."

The present consisted (1) of one single ruby made into a cup, about half a foot high, an inch thick, and filled with round pearls of half a dram each. (2) The skin of a serpent, whose scales were as bright as an ordinary piece of gold, and had the virtue to preserve from sickness those who lay upon it. (3) Fifty thousand drams of the best wood of aloes, with thirty grains of camphor as big as pistachios. And (4) a female slave of great beauty, whose robe was covered with jewels.

The ship set sail, and after a very successful navigation we landed at Bussorah, and from thence I went to the city of Bagdad, where the first thing I did was to acquit myself of my commission.

I took the King of Serendib's letter, and went to present myself at the gate of the Commander of the Faithful, and was immediately conducted to the throne of the caliph. I made my obeisance, and presented the letter and gift. When he had read what the King of Serendib wrote to him, he asked me if that prince were really so rich and potent as he represented himself in his letter. I prostrated myself a second time, and rising again, said, "Commander of the Faithful, I can assure your majesty he doth not exceed the truth. I bear him witness. Nothing is more worthy of admiration than the magnificence of his palace. When the prince appears in public, he has a throne fixed on the back of an elephant, and rides betwixt two ranks of his ministers, favorites, and other people of his court. Before him, upon the same elephant, an officer carries a golden lance in his hand; and behind him there is another, who stands with a rod of gold, on the top of which is an emerald, half a foot long and an inch thick. He is attended by a guard of one thousand men, clad in cloth of gold and silk, and mounted on elephants richly caparisoned. The officer who is before him on the same elephant, cries from time to time, with a loud voice, 'Behold the great monarch, the potent and redoubtable Sultan of the Indies, the monarch greater than Solomon, and the powerful Maharaja.' After he has pronounced those words, the officer behind the throne cries, in his turn, 'This monarch, so great and so powerful, must die, must die, must die.' And the officer before replies, 'Praise alone be to Him who liveth forever and ever.'"

The caliph was much pleased with my account, and sent me home with a rich present.

Here Sindbad commanded another hundred sequins to be paid to Hindbad, and begged his return on the morrow to hear his seventh and last voyage.

The Seventh and Last Voyage Of Sindbad the Sailor

On my return home from my sixth voyage I had entirely given up all thoughts of again going to sea; for, besides that my age now required rest, I was resolved no more to expose myself to such risks as I had encountered, so that I thought of nothing but to pass the rest of my days in tranquillity. One day, however, an officer of the caliph's inquired for me.

"The caliph," said he, "has sent me to tell you that he must speak with you."

I followed the officer to the palace, where, being presented to the caliph, I saluted him by prostrating myself at his feet.

"Sindbad," said he to me, "I stand in need of your service; you must carry my answer and present to the King of Serendib."

This command of the caliph was to me like a clap of thunder. "Commander of the Faithful," I replied, "I am ready to do whatever your majesty shall think fit to command; but I beseech you most humbly to consider what I have undergone. I have also made a vow never to leave Bagdad."

Perceiving that the caliph insisted upon my compliance, I submitted, and told him that I was willing to obey. He was very well pleased, and ordered me one thousand sequins for the expenses of my journey.

I prepared for my departure in a few days. As soon as the caliph's letter and present were delivered to me, I went to

Bussorah, where I embarked, and had a very prosperous voyage. Having arrived at the Isle of Serendib, I was conducted to the palace with much pomp, when I prostrated myself on the ground before the king.

"Sindbad," said the king, "you are welcome. I have many times thought of you; I bless the day on which I see you once more."

I made my compliments to him, and thanked him for his kindness, and delivered the gifts from my august master.

The caliph's letter was as follows:

"Greeting, in the name of the Sovereign Guide of the Right Way, from the servant of God, Haroun al Raschid, whom God hath set in the place of vice-regent to His Prophet, after his ancestors of happy memory, to the potent and esteemed Raja of Serendib.

"We received your letter with joy, and send you this from our imperial residence, the garden of superior wits. We hope, when you look upon it, you will perceive our good intention, and be pleased with it. Farewell."

The caliph's present was a complete suit of cloth of gold, valued at one thousand sequins; fifty robes of rich stuff, a hundred of white cloth, the finest of Cairo, Suez, and Alexandria; a vessel of agate, more broad than deep, an inch thick, and half a foot wide, the bottom of which represented in bas-relief a man with one knee on the ground, who held a bow and an arrow, ready to discharge at a lion. He sent him also a rich tablet, which, according to tradition, belonged to the great Solomon.

The King of Serendib was highly gratified at the caliph's acknowledgment of his friendship. A little time after this audience I solicited leave to depart, and with much difficulty obtained it. The king, when he dismissed me, made me a very considerable present. I embarked immediately to return to Bagdad, but had not the good fortune to arrive there so speedily as I had hoped. God ordered it otherwise.

Three or four days after my departure we were attacked by pirates, who easily seized upon our ship because it was not a vessel of war. Some of the crew offered resistance, which cost them their lives. But for myself and the rest, who were not so imprudent, the pirates saved us, and carried us into a remote island, where they sold us.

I fell into the hands of a rich merchant, who, as soon as he bought me, took me to his house, treated me well, and clad me handsomely as a slave. Some days after, he asked me if I understood any trade. I answered that I was no mechanic, but a merchant, and that the pirates who sold me had robbed me of all I possessed.

"Tell me," replied he, "can you shoot with a bow?"

I answered, that the bow was one of my exercises in my youth. He gave me a bow and arrows, and taking me behind him on an elephant, carried me to a thick forest some leagues from the town. We penetrated a great way into the wood, and when he thought fit to stop, he bade me alight; then showing me a great tree, "Climb up that," said he, "and shoot at the elephants as you see them pass by, for there is a prodigious number of them in this forest, and if any of them fall come and give me notice."

Having spoken thus, he left me victuals, and returned to the town, and I continued upon the tree all night.

I saw no elephant during the night, but next morning, at break of day, I perceived a great number. I shot several arrows among them; and at last one of the elephants fell, when the rest retired immediately, and left me at liberty to go and acquaint my patron with my success. When I had informed him, he commended my dexterity, and caressed me highly. We went afterward together to the forest, where we dug a hole for the elephant, my patron designing to return when it was rotten, and take his teeth to trade with.

I continued this employment for two months. One morning, as I looked for the elephants, I perceived with extreme amazement that, instead of passing by me across the forest as usual, they stopped, and came to me with a horrible noise, and in such numbers that the plain was covered and shook under them. They surrounded the tree in which I was concealed, with their trunks uplifted, and all fixed their eyes upon me. At this alarming spectacle I continued immovable, and was so much terrified that my bow and arrows fell out of my hand.

My fears were not without cause; for after the elephants had stared upon me some time, one of the largest of them put his trunk round the foot of the tree, plucked it up, and threw it on the ground. I fell with the tree, and the elephant, taking me up with his trunk, laid me on his back, where I sat more like one dead than alive, with my quiver on my shoulder. He put himself at the head of the rest, who followed him in line one after the other, carried me a considerable way, then laid me down on the ground, and retired with all his companions. After having lain some time, and seeing the elephants gone, I got up, and found I was upon a long and broad hill, almost covered with the bones and teeth of elephants. I doubted not but that this was the burial place of the elephants, and that they carried me thither on purpose to tell me that I should forbear to kill them, as now I knew where to get their teeth without inflicting injury on them. I did not stay on the hill, but turned toward the city; and after having traveled a day and a night, I came to my patron.

As soon as my patron saw me, "Ah, poor Sindbad," exclaimed he, "I was in great trouble to know what was become of you. I have been to the forest, where I found a tree newly pulled up, and your bow and arrows on the ground, and I despaired of ever seeing you more. Pray tell me what befell you."

I satisfied his curiosity, and we both of us set out next morning to the hill. We loaded the elephant which had carried us with as many teeth as he could bear; and when we were returned, my master thus addressed me: "Hear now what I shall tell you. The elephants of our forest have every year killed us a great many slaves, whom we sent to seek ivory. For all the cautions we could give them, these crafty animals destroyed them one time or other. God has delivered you from their fury, and has bestowed that favor upon you only. It is a sign that He loves you, and has some use for your service in the world. You have procured me incredible wealth; and now our whole city is enriched by your means, without any more exposing the lives of our slaves. After such a discovery, I can treat you no more as a slave, but as a brother. God bless you with all happiness and prosperity. I henceforth give you your liberty; I will also give you riches."

To this I replied, "Master, God preserve you. I desire no other reward for the service I had the good fortune to do to you and your city, but leave to return to my own country."

"Very well," said he, "the monsoon will in a little time bring ships for ivory. I will then send you home."

I stayed with him while waiting for the monsoon; and during that time we made so many journeys to the hill that we filled all our warehouses with ivory. The other merchants who traded in it did the same; for my master made them partakers of his good fortune.

The ships arrived at last, and my master himself having made choice of the ship wherein I was to embark, loaded half of it with ivory on my account, laid in provisions in abundance for my passage, and besides obliged me to accept a present of some curiosities of the country of great value. After I had returned him a thousand thanks for all his favors, I went aboard.

We stopped at some islands to take in fresh provisions. Our vessel being come to a port on the mainland in the Indies, we touched there, and not being willing to venture by sea to Bussorah, I landed my portion of the ivory, resolving to proceed on my journey by land. I realized vast sums by my ivory, bought several rarities, which I intended for presents, and when my equipage was ready, set out in company with a large caravan of merchants. I was a long time on the journey, and suffered much, but was happy in thinking that I had nothing to fear from the seas, from pirates, from serpents, or from the other perils to which I had been exposed.

I at last arrived safe at Bagdad, and immediately waited upon the caliph, to give him an account of my embassy. He loaded me with honors and rich presents, and I have ever since devoted myself to my family, kindred, and friends.

Sindbad here finished the relation of his seventh and last voyage, and then addressing himself to Hindbad, "Well, friend," said he, "did you ever hear of any person that suffered so much as I have done? Is it not reasonable that, after all this, I should enjoy a quiet and pleasant life?"

As he said these words, Hindbad kissed his hand, and said, "Sir, my afflictions are not to be compared with yours. You not only deserve a quiet life but are worthy of all the riches you possess, since you make so good a use of them. May you live happily for a long time."

Sindbad ordered him to be paid another hundred sequins, and told him to give up carrying burdens as a porter, and to eat henceforth at his table, for he wished that he should all his life have reason to remember that he henceforth had a friend in Sindbad the sailor.

CPSIA information can be obtained
at www.ICGtesting.com
Printed in the USA
BVHW070017090223
658191BV00023B/595